"When is the next book out?"
(Almost everyone I meet. Thanks ☺)

"Why are you talking to me?"
(Random person at the bus stop)

"What were you doing on an electric scooter? Don't you know we're in the midst of a global pandemic."
(Family, Friends and Health Care Professionals)

"I am so pleased Jen's story continues. Her quirky outlook and sideways glance at the world distracts from the ongoing sense of impending doom."
(Hamish, aged 4)

Dedicated to the wonderful team at St. John's Hospital who provided a high standard of care and compassion when I hit my own literal bump in the road.

Thank you too to all my kind readers for your words of encouragement and continued support.

A Bump in the Road

Written by
Gillian Lee Gibson

CHAPTER 1

This isn't Armageddon. This isn't Armageddon.

I mean, sure, the sky's burning black and red from the flames and I'm confident hooves can be heard above the screaming of sirens but, this isn't Armageddon. *Not again. Deep breaths, Jen. This is just...*

"F-ing arson." Neil handed me a cup of tea. "Extra sugar. For the shock."

"I'm not in shock." Although my hands couldn't feel the warmth of the cup in the cold night air and we were standing so close to the flames my cheeks should have been burning. Yet, I felt nothing. Numb.

The sign 'Woodfield Community Centre' fell from the building. Neil took my hand, as though this moment was more significant than any of the others.

"It's gone, Jen." He whispered as his eyes frantically scanned the crowd.

"Who are you looking for?" I challenged. Neil was being more annoying than usual.

Neil looked disappointed. "Just junkies and the homeless out at this time of night."

"Right, your peeps." I mocked. "Who were you expecting?"

"How was dinner?" He asked, as though anything else but this fire mattered.

"It was in that new Hipster place up town. Loads of people seen me."

Neil looked briefly confused as I laid out my alibi for the night.

I wasn't here when the fire started. *I ain't going down for this one, Gov.* What? Too soon? Blame the sleep deprivation.

"The whole experience was crap."

People didn't have dinner anymore. They had experiences and documented it all on social media.

"If you're at all interested in the answer."

Neil had drifted off. Again.

"I'm sorry I had to wake you."

He should have been sorry not to have called sooner.

"I wasn't asleep." I was in bed, alone.

"What's your alibi? And, more importantly, who can corroborate it?" I wanted not to think about tonight.

On more than one occasion Neil and I had threatened to torch this place. Usually with our enemies in it. That's just how you pass the time at work, right?

"We won't need an alibi." He stammered.

I disagreed. Neil and I would be top of the list of suspects.

When Neil phoned I thought it was a joke. The standard 'something bad has happened' call to get me out of dinner with the evil step-daughter and her satanic offspring. Unfortunately not. Neil had forgotten his earlier intervention was required. Dinner had gone undisturbed. Well, that's not quite true. All interactions with that less than dynamic duo were disturbing. Only, Neil hadn't lost track of time. Like when he hilariously rocked up for work in the summer 12 hours early. This time something bad really had happened. Although, when Neil had called to say that our place of work was ablaze, it almost came as light relief.

"Caitlin still being a bitch?" Neil tried to focus on our discussion.

"Don't call her that." At least, not within Ron's ear shot.

"She's just taken a while to adjust." I added weakly.

Neil snorted.

"It couldn't even have been burning that long." Fire was tearing through the building. Large chunks of walls just fell to ash. The emergency services kept trying to push the crowd back as more and more people arrived to witness and photograph the horror. The smart phone generation were out in force. They probably began videoing the destruction well before anyone thought to call the Fire Brigade.

"It's a shame none of them used the place when it was open." As the flames danced in his eyes I thought I saw the glimmer of tears.

"I thought you were joking." I could barely hear my voice above the roar of the fire and the wail of the sirens. Smoke burnt the back of my throat.

"You thought I'd fallen off the wagon." Neil had sworn off alcohol since 'the incident'. Solemnly telling that woman in HR he realised, 'alcohol isn't the answer'. It kinda depends on the question though, doesn't it? Neil's been sober for three months. The longest twelve weeks of my life. And, last year, I'd been declared bankrupt and had to move back in with my parents. I thought 2017 was going to be the worst year of my life. Apparently historians will look back on that and laugh.

"I must not drink." Neil took a deep breath and pretended to be strong. I nodded and pretended to be sympathetic but, I'm pretty sure I just looked annoyed. Neil didn't have a drinking problem. He didn't really have any problems. That's why he had to invent them. It might be a good time to remind him his ex-girlfriend had just given birth to her cousin's baby and, to add insult to injury, they called it 'Sunshine'.

"Just say it," I whispered. If anything warranted the f-bomb it was this. Neil's 'swear jar' would be consumed by fire too. None of it mattered now. I resented that in the chaos he'd found and stuck to a new calm. Neil insisted on 'managing' the situation. That seemed to involve harassing the fire fighters at a time they were otherwise occupied. Although he had three phone numbers and the promise of a curry so what did I know?

Maybe this was his extreme attempt to find a life partner. Or a turbulent three month partner that went from love, to hate and back to love before the inevitable blocking on all forms of social media and ritualistic burning of any possessions left at his home. I looked at Neil again with suspicion. Fire was his go to catharsis.

"Why are you looking at me like that?" Neil's eyes stopped scanning the crowd.

People always say when something terrible happens time slows down. Not that it gives you an opportunity to intervene, just more of a chance to watch your life fall apart. The lovely new Community Centre and my brilliant job, were disappearing before my eyes - and all I could do, was watch.

This isn't Armageddon. This isn't Armageddon.

Ron cleared his throat I'd forgotten he was there. This was like a dream. A nightmare. I screwed up my eyes. Any moment now I would wake up.

Anxiety scorched Ron's face. "You're sure this had nothing to do with you?"

It wasn't funny the first time he said it.

CHAPTER 2

Fairy tales usually end with a wedding. Mine ended in a Leisure Centre in a deprived part of town. I'd chumba wumbaed like a legend (you know - got knocked down and got back up again). I used to call it My Own Little Personal Armageddon. Just in case you think I'm being a tad melodramatic (because, apparently, I can be) here's a quick summary. My then boyfriend (Stephen) ran off with all my money, leaving me with a ton of debt and minus my beloved bookshop. My flat had to be sold. I moved back in with my parents and fell in love (with my new boss, Ron). Unfortunately, it turned out Ron had foreclosed on the business loan that made me homeless, so I dumped him. Then, after finding a new job teaching adults to read, getting all my money back (because Stephen turned up and my insurance company 'made it rain'), I got life back together but, try as I might, I couldn't get over Ron. We've been living together for over six months. Armageddon well and truly over. There wasn't a cloud in the sky. Life was tra la la la perfect. I could be a motivations speaker. I was ready to change the world. Now my life was sorted it was only right I should take some time out of relationship bliss and help others... Only... OK, perhaps there were a few little clouds on the horizon. One of which was the smouldering remains of the Community Centre.

"So you understand?" Coronary Chris wheezed his way to the end of the sentence.

Well, you are speaking English. Sort of. Some kind of management speak, not unlike English but I got the gist. 'Going forward' they had to make 'efficiencies' and given that my place of work no longer existed they couldn't be paying me to watch daytime TV. I understood, at least, I was again unemployed. The first little cloud, but I wasn't going to let it get me down. I had a new outlook on life. It was good I'd been paid off. Freed me up for more meaningful endeavours. Only, it had been two weeks since the Centre burned down and I'd done nothing. Literally nothing. One day I'd actually started counting the hairs on my left arm because (get this) it seemed hairier than the right. I needed a job. I was going slowly around the twist and I had a horrible feeling I was taking Ron with me.

No, that's ridiculous. Ron loved me and my quirky ways. He didn't particularly like the hairy arm chart and apparently the picture updates 'freaked him right out' but it's important we share our hobbies.

"What about the insurance?" I liked my job. Well, I hated it less than the others. Besides, I was employed by the Council. They had hundreds of hangers on. I was staring at one of them.

The very fact that Coronary Chris was the Head of Sport and Leisure was absolute proof of the Council's highly developed sense of irony. I know you shouldn't judge a book by its cover, and we're all fighting our own little battles but, you know sometimes judging by appearance just saves time. My first ever contact with Coronary Chris was over the phone. With all the heavy breathing I thought I was on the receiving end of a dirty phone call. I was giving it three more minutes then hanging up. I'd contemplated blowing a whistle down the line. That would have taught him. I'm just not sure what.

I hated that Neil poked such fun at his weight. He'd defended the crass nickname by stating Chris had been categorically told by his doctor to lose weight. Instead, he joked about the heart attacks and boasted about his private medical care. People found it hard to like Chris and, because of that, the nickname just stuck. I tried not to be part of it.

"I could work here." I offered. It wasn't my first choice. It wasn't even in my top ten but unemployed Jen could be a bit of a liability.

Chris spluttered. It was often hard to know when he was reacting to something you'd said and when he was having a medical emergency. He always seemed to be on the cusp of one.

The Woodbank Leisure Centre he'd chosen for our meeting was only a few miles down the road from Woodfield. It was a much older building and rumours were abound that this place would eventually close. The staff here smiled sympathetically when I was shown into the manager's office. The Formica tiles may have been hanging from the ceiling, and exposing us all to asbestos, but with the demise of Woodfield this place had been given a stay of execution.

"What about adult literacy?"

Chris shrugged. "We didn't really have time to get the program up and running. Maybe we'll try again in a few years' time."

"Years?"

He waved his hand dismissively as though improving outcomes of the community wasn't his exact job description.

"We just needed more time." I appealed.

More time and fewer barriers. Chris just wanted an easy life.

Chris had a chain of non-existent jobs before this one. No-one was really sure what he did, or why he was qualified to do it. Neil and I looked him up on LinkedIn. They say a picture speaks a thousand words. Well, that one told a few porkies. His profile picture was at least eight stone and three heart attacks ago.

Chris had worked the length and breadth of the UK. Never staying longer than 18 months in the one place. His profile described him as 'driven'. Back in the real world that's about the time it takes for people to find out the Emperor is not only stark bollock naked but, probably a bit of a tool.

Neil and I, by comparison, worked hard. Most of the time. There was the occasional break to write whimsical songs. My personal favourite was the Proclaimers' Mash up of 'Letters from America' aka 'P45s from the Council'. It provided a thorough breakdown of Chris 'building blocks to success'. The career pathway that made him uniquely qualified for whatever it was he was supposed to be doing now. *Manchester no more, Bradford no more... When you go, Won't you take, A Golden Hand Shake for Birmingham.* We were planning a compilations CD for when Chris left, or, you know, to be played at his memorial service - whichever cames first. We could offer it to him now as a leaving gift. He could put it on Linked-in.

Neil and I had often fantasised about how we'd give our notice. Stapling my resignation (a sticky note with 'I quit' written on it) to Chris forehead was my go to. Neil had laughed, 'Sort of like nailing jelly to the wall. Only, he's the jelly'. That felt like such a long time ago. Back in the days when Neil was capable of laugher. I doubt I'd see much of him now. Neil and I started as 'proximity pals'. Thrown together last year in my endless encounters with the Job Centre. Reunited again after his 'little episode' sent him to Woodfield Community Leisure Centre in some ill-defined role. We bonded, as most adults do, over our mutual hatred of work colleagues, aka Chris.

Today was full of disappointments. In my fantasy exit meetings I had been sitting here dressed as Wonder

Woman, or at least on a throne and wearing a crown. Today, caught me by surprise. Today I didn't know I was leaving.

"What about Neil?" I whispered.

Chris cleared his throat again. "That's confidential."

I had initially tried to like Chris. My cousin Carol had taken an instant dislike to him. 'He's obese'. She sounded genuinely appalled when she'd caught sight of him six months ago at the 'meet and greet'. Carol and Chris were at opposite ends of the fitness spectrum. That reassured me I wasn't 'fattist' (in the sense that I discriminate against the larger person). Carol is a size eight and I don't much like her either.

'He still smokes! Who does that now?' Carol hissed with more than a touch of envy in her voice. Carol used to smoke too. She stopped because she knew it was terrible for her health and the health of everyone else around her but Carol would sell each and every one of us into slavery for a cigarette. She hated Chris for smoking but she would often be standing behind him, inhaling deeply, when he did.

Chris coughed again. I wasn't sure whether he was trying to bring me back to the present or whether it was a sign his vital organs were failing.

'We need to be more body positive as a society.' I had objected.

'Jen.' Carol had taken that patient tone that indicated I hadn't understood the complexity of an issue. 'Chris is putting himself at risk of heart attacks and strokes. You

17

might not care about the bloke but you'll be the one picking up the slack at work'.

I wouldn't. He did nothing. Like, literally, nothing.

"Thank you for coming." Chris wheezed. AKA 'you can piss off now'.

Unemployed. I tried again to process the word. I thought I'd at least outlast Chris.

When he was first appointed I too was fresh in the job. Younger and more full of hope I tried to be compassionate. I wanted to be hopeful about his appointment at the introductory party (well I felt like I should) but it was a tossup between Coronary Chris and Cretin Chris for his office nickname. Neither are names you'd give a friend.

'He's happy,' I'd protested, although I had nothing but speculation to base that on. I could only surmise that someone who ate that much cake in a day would have to be happy. Besdies, I was trying to be nicer to losers. One of the reasons I'd invited Carol to the 'meet and greet'.

'Morbidly happy.' Carol smirked. 'With your history of sleeping with the boss I bet old Ron's bricking it.'

That was the other reason Carol was invited as my plus one to the event.   I tried to keep my relationship with Ron on the 'down low'. Ironic, as my relationship with Ron was probably the only reason I was invited. It's not that I was embarrassed. Everyone gets fed up hearing how wonderful couplehood is. Honestly, sometimes even I want to stab my smug self in the eye.

I knew that I had to make a career for me. Loads of people wanted to be my friend to get 'access to Ron'. I say that with some confidence because I am reliably informed I'm the human equivalent of Marmite.

Carol, Neil and I had watched in horror as Chris puffed and wheezed his way around the crowded Leisure Centre hall. Shaking hands, awkwardly, with staff and the public alike. I was terrified; I still hadn't done the required First Aid module and it was the first time I realised why I might need it.

The 'party' had been held at Woodfield to 'show case' our centre. We had thought/hoped that would be the last we'd see of Chris until the inevitable email, 'We're sad to announce....' Only, Chris had developed an unhealthy interest in our Centre from the start. Despite his endless interference, sorry, intervention, there were more people in the Centre at Chris's 'party' than in the few months that followed. Chris was reluctant to 'move' on any idea despite his reported 'drive'. He'd 'put that on pause' and seemed to almost encourage Neil and I to slack off. Chris was probably only in his late forties. Yet, he was coasting along nicely to retirement. Chris hadn't made that much of an impression since that night. It was hard to gauge if he was effective at his job. He'd often put his hand in front of his mouth before he spoke for complete deniability.

"The insurance," I began.

"The insurance could take years to come through." Chris stood up, or tried to. He wanted me to leave before he actually had to make it to his feet. Neil had timed him once. Five minutes to stand. Then four more for the panting to cease. I was anxious about him standing too. Turns out the First Aid module didn't cover much.

"I don't know a lot about insurance but, that didn't sound right." *They just want rid of you*.

"I was doing a good job." The words came out weaker than I expected. Honestly, of all the jobs I should have been sacked from, this wasn't one of them. I tried really hard.

"You should have done the fire safety training," Chris snarled.

"I wasn't even there!"

"No, but," Chris wheezed, "I told you four times to do that training."

He emailed because, you know, that's what the council pay him 70k a year - to remind people what mandatory training still needs to be completed. I think the Council actually had an App for that.

"You know what you said?" Chris leaned forward menacingly in his seat.

I was joking!

"I probably started it," he quoted, "so I'd have a plan."

CHAPTER 3

It's strange to think that in all the time we'd spent together, Chris and I had never really bonded. People usually warm up to me, in the end. I'd tried to be welcoming and accommodating, at least at first.

"'Why are you here again?" I'm not saying I succeeded.

By week three of Chris almost constant presence, tolerance at Woodfield was wearing a bit thin.

"I like to work at the grass roots level." Chris had set himself up at my desk again. I knew it was some kind of power play. A tactic I'd imagined he'd read in a book. A book probably written in crayon by a demented world leader.

"Hm." Was all I could muster in response. I was fed up getting it in the neck from the 'grass rooters' about how much Chris was paid. Chris was always hanging around offering unhelpful advice. People hated him. I tried not to hate him but only because that kind of emotion took energy and I didn't think he was worth it.

"Well, there's a kid just been sick in the pool. You could go help with that."

He couldn't.

"It's a bit below my pay grade." Chris would churn that out at every opportunity. Often to people who were paid to do what he was refusing to. Neil would never say it but I knew that was the reason he targeted Chris appearance; it felt like the only thing that meant anything to him.

'"The higher up the trees the more monkeys." Sometimes things like that would just fly out my mouth. I actually quite like monkeys.

"Might eat the vom." Neil quipped in a stage whisper that could be heard in a hurricane.

"You were late again this morning." Chris looked at me accusingly.

I wasn't. I just hadn't been as early as him.

"I killed a hobo in my car. It took time to dig the shallow grave and dispose of the body".

Chris frowned at the array of dirty mugs (all of which were his). "I believe you killed someone. I don't believe you tidied up afterwards."

Neil had taken on the mug issue last week. He'd placed signs around the office asking, 'what did your last slave die of?' with pictures of all the offending items. I'd written; 'a poor attitude. Was the bloody cups.' Neil didn't think it was funny. Neil didn't seem to think anything was funny anymore.

"It feels like we're on special measures." Neil stared daggers into Chris back as he left the room. Chris was off to the artisan coffee shop. "Christ will be back before he is."

It seemed that Chris completed his working day before ours even began.

Following 'the incident' at the Job Centre, the Council thought it best to keep Neil away from people. It was quiet here. Quieter than the Council had anticipated. Still, on the plus side I managed to catch up on the daytime soaps and Neil had become a real ace at Badminton.

"I said the same when Ron used to hang around our office." I smiled at the memory of my time at Smiths. That's how bad all of this was getting; I longed for the days in finance.

"Maybe Chris fancies you." Neil whispered then laughed so hard he had to leave the room.

Neil had become obsessed with the idea that Chris was watching him and waiting for him to slip up but, I'd been there three months and I wasn't sure what Neil was supposed to be doing either. Neil was starting to come over a little paranoid. Three weeks before he'd actually come in wearing a tinfoil hat. Sure, Hippy-Crack-Mac (the friendly homeless drug addict who hung around the bins at the back) had given it to him when he unlocked the Centre that morning but, it was 10:30am when I rocked up and he was still wearing it.

"What about you?" Chris looked me up and down on his return. It wasn't leery but it didn't exactly make me feel comfortable. He wheezed his way to the kettle. Our coffee wasn't good enough of course but, he'd made a massive dent in it anyway.

"I heard old Ron's thinking about retiring. I'd have thought you would have bigger plans than this."

I scowled at Neil as he tried to return to the office. Of course Neil couldn't keep his bitch trap shut about my relationship with Ron. Ron wasn't thinking about retiring but I wasn't telling Chris anything. I didn't like him.

Neil picked raisins from his fruit bun and looked at me confused. 'Did you want this?'

I wasn't sure those were raisins. I shook my head, remembering the rat we thought we'd seen last week. Maybe I should have had bigger ambitions than this.

"He's kicking sixty now, isn't he?" Chris continued. He would have known, like anyone else, Ron was my kryptonite.

"Fifty seven." I'd no idea why I responded. It was none of his business how old Ron was.

Chris sneered. "At what point does the older man just become an old man?" He held up his hands in mock surrender. "Oh, I am sorry. Feminists don't want to hear their man's so rich they don't need to work."

For Chris feminism had all gone a bit too far. Which meant, even with his wads of cash he couldn't get a date because, you know, he'd open his mouth and say stuff like that. For me feminism won't have gone far enough until men like him are put in cannons and fired into the sun.

"I'm not a feminist, actually. I'm pretty anti suffragette. Having rights. Having to vote. Bloody political correctness gone mad."

Chris ignored the bait. For a man who was fiercely guarded of his own personal life he was eager to open up ours for dissection at every given opportunity. Initially I had thought it was his crass attempt to make friends. Then, I felt there was something more sinister at play. Ok, so I know I was beginning to sound paranoid too. I'd be asking Neil for a loan of his tinfoil hat soon!

"Would you be as taken with Ron if he was poor?" Chris smiled wryly, as though he had me figured out.

Ha! I'd lived inside this head for 28 (ahem) years and I hadn't a clue. I'd spent two hours thinking about whether I could have a pet llama and addressing more practical issues, like where I'd keep it. I didn't have any kind of a life plan. I just bumble from one life disaster to the next.

Neil thankfully dropped his bun in the bin. I was increasingly sure those weren't currants.

Chris smiled again with a lack of sincerity. "And what do you want from life? You're at that age, aren't you? Will we be hearing the pitter patter of tiny feet?"

"We do most days." I locked eyes with Chis determined not to be intimidated. "I think some of those rats are wearing bloody clogs. Have you dealt with that yet?"

Of course he hadn't. He wouldn't want to wipe out his family. That was unfair. Some of those rats were quite cute. Another thought occurred to me.

"'Legally, I don't think you're allowed to ask me that."

"We were just chatting." Chris sneered. "As friends."

25

"We're not friends." Neil and I said in unison. I wished that I hadn't. I wanted to have next Wednesday off. Feels like that's the kind of thing you would agree to for a friend.

"I would like us to be friends." Chris voice again was insincere. He would like us to think that we were friends so that we could be useful to him; until we weren't.

"Perhaps I can give you some friendly advice." He tried to look as though he would proceed with caution but I felt the next statement too was part of his bigger plan.

"Just be careful, Jen. Old Ron's richer than Midas and, in case you don't know that story, it didn't end well."

CHAPTER 4

'I hope he has a bloody heart attack!' Neil fumed as he watched Chris leave the Community Centre.

"Who was Midas?"

Neil either didn't know or didn't care.

I hoped Chris didn't have a heart attack. If only for the paper work. Someone slipped on a piece of black ice at Christmas and there was a mountain of forms.

"Let him have that long overdue coronary event when he was harassing the staff of Woodbank on a Tuesday and Thursday." Neil placed his hands together in mock prayer but the venom in his voice was potent.

Chris would do it here. Just to inconvenience me.

"Maybe he's lonely."

Mum always said people who are the most unlovable are the ones who need our affection the most.

Neil didn't have time for compassion. He was staring into the bin. He looked as though he was contemplating taking his cake out and eating it.

"Of course he's lonely. People don't have family when they're spawned from rubber."

"You know that bun is covered in rat crap." I shared my suspicions.

"Yeah." Neil didn't look like he cared.

"Why the hell did you tell him about Ron?"

"I didn't."

"Well, someone did." I accused.

"It wasn't me." Neil sounded like a whiney child.

I wanted to point out that no one else spoke to Chris. In fact, with all the cutbacks over the past few months meant there were very few people he could speak to here. Next week the council would be draining the pool so the buff lifeguard Bill had been given his notice too. That may also have accounted for Neil's particularly foul mood. With Buff Bill gone why not eat the rancid cake from the bin? What else was there left to live for?

"Aren't you on the raw diet?" Or some other nonsense that probably didn't include rat faeces. "Wasn't it Buff Bill that told you all about it?"

That was a trick. I knew Neil's mystery man had told him about the diet. I was trying to find out whether the two were one and the same.

Neil gazed at the remnants of the cake. "Shouldn't the rats be deserting this sinking ship rather than hanging around here and wasting good cake?"

"Things not going well with the mystery man?"

Neil had been unusually cagey about his latest sexual conquest. Uncharacteristically discreet. It was bugging the Hell out of me.

"Do I know him?"

He stood up and brushed the crumbs from his desk.

"Maybe that's what happened to Chris. One heartbreak too many." I tried to open up a cautionary tale about bottling up emotion. Neil had known me at my meanest.

"One steak pie too many you mean." He shut the conversation back down.

Neil looked crushed. "Do you think people can change?"

"People, yes. Chris, no. He's a lost cause." I had tried over the months. Oh, how I had tried.

Chris just didn't have enough personal insight. Still, I suppose if I was serious about being a motivational speaker (although I'd forgotten three times already about that plan), I shouldn't write Chris off.

"I suppose if I can change." I still considered myself somewhat of a success story. Although even I noticed the upward inflection of my voice that sounded like a question mark at the end.

"He's a tosser, Jen. An absolute 110% gold carat, tool."

I wasn't sure who we were talking about.

"What's happened now?" I realised it was the wrong question. A clumsy one. When things weren't going well with Stephen I tried to hide it because I hated that question. I hated reminder there was a growing list of reasons why I shouldn't be with him. I hated the pressure that placed on me to change things. I knew from bitter experience people had to come to the end of their own road. So there was no ambiguity; no way back.

"Chris thinks I'm with Ron for his money." I chose to deflect and tried to take some of the judgement away. "Chris thinks Ron's only with me because I'm young, a bit of an ego boost. That's what everyone thinks. Isn't it?" I hadn't intended to sound so truthful.

Neil laughed. "Wow!" He stopped. "You're serious!"

"Forget it." I stood up. I would do the grown-up thing and have a little cry in the toilet but, I hesitated. Neil had seen me through some of the darkest times of my life. He was a reluctant therapist, and he got signed off sick twice, but when you had him in the room he gave some sound advice.

"Ron's working more."

"What?" Neil looked distractedly at his computer. A tactic he used to avoid conversations or 'directives' from Chris.

"He's at the office more and more. Even when he's home he's hauled up in the spare room on his laptop."

"You mean the cupboard you stuck a futon in?" Neil's tone dismissive of not only our home but my concerns.

"Look, Jen." His voice softened. "Not everyone has a job like us."

"Meaning?"

"Meaning when was the last time you took work home?"

"I used too. Now there was barely enough to do during the day." Maybe Ron and I had nothing in common. "What if he's working to fill the void?"

"What void?" Neil massaged his temples and checked his phone for the hundredth time. He wasn't really listening. He'd been distracted for weeks.

"Maybe the novelty of us has worn off." I could see that he wasn't interested and, maybe, because I felt Neil wasn't really listening, it was ok to say my worst fear out loud.

"Ron's with you because..." Neil trailed off.

"Yes?"

"I don't know why the hell he's with you, Jen. Most people, including me, find you pretty bloody irritating."

"Thanks." Back to plan A and the good old cry in the toilets. Maybe I would call Mum. I'd ask her if she was still signed up for the motivational quotes social media page. I would ask if there was anything pertinent to my situation.

"You seem genuinely fond of him and...."

"And?" I prompted.

He shrugged.

"And, I'm sure you'd love him, Jen. Even if he was broke." I offered the reassuring words I wanted to hear.

"Oh yeah," Neil looked less certain. "'Course."

CHAPTER 5

"I was only saying." Caitlin petulantly flicked her peroxide blonde hair from her face and brazened on. Her sharp voice filled the restaurant.

"I just don't think the taxpayer should be held responsible."

It had been the third comment of the evening even the *Daily Mail* would have blushed to print. I hated Caitlin. Not in the whimsical way I used to think I hated my former colleague (now friend) Janice. I properly hated Caitlin. She reminded me of a peacock. Beautiful, mean as hell and absolutely forbidden to kick in the face. Maybe I was being unfair to peacocks with the generalisation. Perhaps it was just that particular peacock on that particular school trip that had been an asshole. Maybe time had even changed that dickhead bird.

"Are you ok?" Ron whispered.

"Do peacocks grow as, I don't know, birds?"

Ron looked more confused. This was the point in the evening where I would pretend I was tired and just quiet; rather than simply stating I had nothing to say or, at least, nothing to say to Caitlin.

Ron's eyes scanned the restaurant for a clue to the latest conversational tangent. Plastic ferns adorned the walls of 'Bullrush', the latest Hipster Hideaway on the South Side of town. A place so fresh it still stank of paint.

"Why are you talking about peacocks?" Ron looked bemused.

"I think the question is why are we not talking about peacocks?"

Caitlin shifted audibly in her chair. Every movement, every utterance pre-mediated for dramatic effect.

Ron turned his attention back to.... How to adequately describe Caitlin without using the word viper? Probably with a strained laugh and a, 'That's just Caitlin.' Subtext, 'She's a bitch but you get used to her'. Or you'll avoid her. At least, you'll try to.

Carol suggested Caitlin was playing hard to get in the friendship stakes. I mean, why bother when you're so hard to like? If I had to list people I hated Caitlin would come before Chris and, I had to make a conscious daily effort just to dislike him.

No Jen, take deep soothing breaths. Imagine walking down a country lane. Dragging her body in a bag and carrying a shovel.

Whoops. That visual meditation got away from me.

"We were lucky to get a table here." I tried to engage again with Caitlin. Just when I thought she couldn't get any more annoying, she had taken to wearing a black Heisenberg hat.

"Luck had nothing to do with it." She sneered. Or perhaps that was her permanent expression now.

For once I had to agree. We were not 'lucky' to get a table in yet another style over substance restaurant. Tiny portions and incomprehensible ingredients. I hoped I was allergic to some of them. Anaphylaxis would be preferrable to this. Of course you'll think me dramatic again but remember it was only a few weeks ago my place of work burnt down and interrupted another evening just like this. That emergency call was a bit of light relief.

"It's all about who you know." Caitlin's voice boomed again.

Ron reached under the table and gently took my hand. He smiled, reassuringly. Caitlin had kept us waiting for a good half hour. Ron seemed relieved when she finally arrived. He kept speculating as to why she had been delayed. I couldn't say what I was really thinking, 'probably had trouble parking her broomstick'.

"What was the hold-up tonight?" Ron inquired.

I don't know why he continued to be surprised. Caitlin often kept us waiting.

Around Caitlin my face had forgotten how to smile. The best I could manage looked more like a snarl. The reflection looking back at me from the mirror across the room didn't even feel like me.

Caitlin sat up defensively. There would be another lecture on not knowing how hard it was to have children. The child would get the blame but, it would be Caitlin's fault. Caitlin would have had several outfit changes, or she would have waited too long to even start getting ready. When meeting Ron and I there was never a time pressure. Caitlin would arrive when she arrived. Ron and I would always have to be early. Some time alone would have been nice. Except waiting for Caitlin produced a similar anticipatory dread as waiting to be seen at the dentist. It wouldn't matter to Caitlin this place was on the opposite side of town for us. Ron and I never featured in her thinking. For Caitlin the fun was in telling people about the event. Not the actual experience and, in a way, she was right about that too. There was no fun to be had here.

"I don't know why I'm being put on trial." Caitlin pouted. A woman in her late twenties, with her own child, properly huffed.

"You're not being put on trial." Ron's tone apologetic.

"But if you really want your day in court you can have mine. I think it's the fourteenth. FYI I'm going to say it was the cough syrup. Potent stuff."

"She's joking." Ron looked less sure than he tried to sound. "I think."

Silence. Well there would have been silence had the feral child not been screeching at the top of his lungs. It was a bloody awful sound that he seemed to have perfected about twenty minutes ago.

"Chris doesn't think you burned the Centre down." Ron spoke quietly. As if the tornado of noise from the devil child was not overpowering any meaningful communication.

I wanted to throw a plate at the wall and scream, 'I can't bloody do this anymore'. Instead, I took a deep breath and fought back the tears.

The smart money was on Hippy-Crack-Mac as the resident arsonist. Don't get me wrong he was never in line to lead the Olympic torch around town, mostly because all the meth in his system meant that it was a bad idea to be that close to a naked flame. Still, I never had him down for an arsonist. Mac liked us at the Centre - I think. He spoke with that distinctive nasal flair of the chemically dependent, so, most of the time it was hard to tell what he was saying, but it didn't have the feel of, 'I'm going to burn that place to the ground'. Even if it did, he wouldn't be physically able. Even I'd outrun Mac.

"Not this again." Caitlin rolled her eyes. "I thought you would be over that by now."

"Over losing my job? Not in a few weeks, no." Caitlin hadn't thought about how I would be feeling. Caitlin was simply over hearing about it.

"I heard they arrested someone." She looked distractedly at the menu. "Do you think the paneer has cumin in it?"

I hoped not.

36

"Some old addict you encouraged to hang around the centre?" She accused.

"Where did you hear that, Caitlin? From whom?" There was only one person who could have said anything and he was shifting awkwardly in his seat. Even in my anger I had to give myself snaps for using the proper pronoun.

"Mac…" I tried to explain the error.

Caitlin cut me off and began talking incessantly about her manicure. You know, the important things in life.

The tiny devil child she'd spawned ran around the restaurant with breadsticks stuck up his nose. Ron looked at me, with an expression I found hard to read. It seemed he was broody. He must also be concussed. The first time I met this pair I'd googled two for one exorcisms; then vasectomies. I used to think I wanted children, then I met one. Or, more specifically, this one. Every time I saw him the theme tune to *The Omen* played in my head.

Caitlin had chosen the restaurant. A swanky establishment with impatient staff who appeared openly hostile to children. Or, again, perhaps just this child. Our fellow diners would be paying hundreds of pounds to endure his antics. The disapproving looks had gone unnoticed by the Smiths. Caitlin, and perhaps even Ron, appeared oblivious to the comments and glares from each and every table. The other diners would be tanking this place on TripAdvisor for their lax attitude to unruly children. It would be closed in a week. Ron and I would be dragged to the next big nothing so Caitlin could brag about the experience to her equally vapid friends. Social media was awash with her dining experiences with 'Daddy'. No mention of Jen. Ever.

I tried catching the eye of the others in the restaurant but, they viewed us all with equal disdain. In their minds I was part of the problem. Maybe they were right. I sat here too and said nothing. All it takes for evil to prosper is for good people to do nothing. Maybe now I was too far in. I wasn't one of the good people anymore.

Large mirrors clung to every wall, intertwined with the ferns. They reflected back light and hurt my eyes but, they reflected something else too. Something I didn't want to see. An image of me. A shadowy figure I hadn't looked at properly in weeks. There was something about my reflection that disturbed me. Something more than the weight I'd gained. Something everyone here should have noticed before the antics of the lead in the remake of the *Village of the Damned*. Sadness. I looked so sad. So sad it physically hurt. I hadn't felt this bad in a very long time.

Caitlin looked behind her. In my mind her head rotated 360 degrees. "What are you looking at?"

"I...." I tried to regain my voice but what could I say? 'I'm looking at the shadow I've become and trying to work out whether it was you or me that did this'.

It felt like all we ever did now was have excruciating dinners with Caitlin and *Rosemary's Child*. I could feel tears sting my eyes.

"Sorry." I grabbed a napkin. "Allergies."

"The ferns were flown over specially from Cambodia." Caitlin basked in the perceived opulence of her surroundings (although I had seen ferns like that in IKEA last week).

I turned away from the mirror, but there were others, all around. I pulled up my handbag from the floor.

"I bought Joey a little colour-in pack." Last time I had tried that trick he ate the crayons but, I was grateful for an excuse to hide my face for a few seconds as I fumbled in my bag. Crying in front of Caitlin would be the ultimate sign of weakness.

"Do you know the environmental impact of that tat?" Caitlin looked at the gift with disdain.

Funny, I often thought the same thing when I looked at her.

"Probably a bit less than flying plastic ferns from Cambodia."

Ron squeezed my hand, reigning me back in.

Joey's high-pitched scream, amplified by the mirrors, filled the restaurant. For a second I thought it was me.

"Sorry." The apology slipped out.

Ron and Cailtin looked at me confused.

"Jen," his voice softened at my name. "Are you sure you're ok?"

I wondered if it was acceptable to claim to be unwell and need to go home. Only, I knew Ron would come too and then, he would fuss and Caitlin would fume. The next meeting would then be even worse.

"Are you looking forward to St. Raphael?" I changed the subject.

Catlin and Craig spent the month of September in the South of France. I'd been looking forward to it for weeks. Probably more than they were.

"We're not going this year," Caitlin snipped. "Some of us are worried about our carbon footprint."

"You can offset it." Hell, I'd plant trees for the rest of the year if it meant four weeks without that pair of assholes.

"You'll be relieved." Caitlin looked accusingly at Ron.

"I'm sorry that you'll be missing your holiday."

His compassion inflamed her more.

"I mean, you'll be glad that she isn't working in that place anymore."

I wanted to shout that she had a name. If only to remind myself. To remind Ron too. As usual, he was letting all of this just happen.

"That area has a terrible crime rate." Caitlin blazoned on. "That Centre was like the gateway to Hell. I know you never liked her working there."

If anyone knew where the gate to Hell was, it would be Satan's concubine. Hang on.

"What do you mean, Ron doesn't like me working there?"

"I...." Ron looked at Caitlin, then me.

"You showed me that article about all those muggings. They had to put extra CCTV around the cash points." Caitlin laughed. "As if any of them have money.

That must have been for you." Caitlin looked at me accusingly. Another insinuation I was bleeding her father dry when this dinner was likely to cost more than our mortgage this month.

"Isn't he darling?" Caitlin turned her attention to little Lucifer before we had a chance to respond. She watched as Chucky offered the bogey-soaked breadstick to unsuspecting diners. One guy, not realising where it had been, actually ate it. I felt sick. Clearly the mothering gene had passed me by or this was evolution at work; removing my genes from the pool. I didn't point out the obvious – that the entire restaurant had grown tired of her spawn's antics.

Ron loves them.

No, Ron has some form of Stockholm Syndrome where he thinks he loves them. I'll have him deprogrammed next week.

The trouble with having had your own little Armageddon is it makes you more compassionate. Or, at least, you understand it should make you more compassionate. You realise everyone is fighting a battle the world knows nothing about. So you tolerate their off days with patience, understanding and just the slightest urge to stab them in the eye with a pencil. This new-found Zen helped repress the urge to quip whenever we met: 'If you're here, who's guarding Hades?' Well, that and the inconvenient truth that Caitlin is Ron's daughter.

"Remember when I was that size, Daddy?" Caitlin smiled, excluding me again from the conversation. She

41

looked fondly at Chucky. Or, at least, I think it was fondness in her eyes. I've never seen anything close to affection looking back at me. So, it was hard to tell. Ron smiled too. Maybe Caitlin was nice before life got to her. Perhaps she was different when alone with her father.

"Remember that Christmas. All I wanted was a Furby? Mummy asked you to bring one back from New York. It was the only time she ever trusted you with anything so important."

Ron looked to the floor.

"I cried for a week when Santa didn't bring one. I don't think I ever really got over it. I think that was the year I stopped believing in Santa. And miracles."

Bloody Hell. That was dark. Even for me.

"It was the year Laura got sick." Ron held my hand tighter.

"I'm sorry." That was my role here. To keep apologising to Caitlin for things that weren't my fault.

"Weren't Furbies those little demonic things that spoke?" I recalled the little mechanical fiends and understood why Caitlin would have been attracted to such an item. "They were pretty creepy."

Caitlin glowered. "It was all I ever wanted."

I found that hard to believe.

"Bet you had one too, Jen. We're about the same age, aren't we?"

"Yeah," I sighed. "They were really hard to get . Fortunately my Dad bought one last minute off some bloke coming back from New York."

Caitlin sneered. "Its weird to think you were playing with Furbies when Daddy was already married with a child."

It's weird to hear a grown woman call her Dad, Daddy.

"I suppose, if we'd met then, people could have an opinion on it."

"I'm not just people." Caitlin growled.

Caitlin is younger than me; just. Although, like any parent, she plays the smug 'life experience' card. Well, she used to. Until I told her that was my mother's euphemism for her cousin who'd been on the game. I'd also had to explain being 'on the game' meant prostitution. We lived in such different worlds.

"How's Joey enjoying Nursery?" Ron tried to change the subject.

Joey (spawn of Satan) had been attending 'Moonbeams' (which I am not entirely sure isn't a branch of Scientology) in preparation for Caitlin going back to work. I'm gutted she'd decided against being a stay-at-home parent. It's been funny watching her slow descent into madness from attending a never-ending stream of Mother and Toddler events. Caitlin was fanatical that little Joey should 'have the best start in life' (with the clear implication that her own left some room for improvement). Probably should have opted for adoption or to let him be raised by wolves in the wild.

You'd have thought Ron's grandson would have been safer ground for conversation. It was far more emotionally charged since 'the misunderstanding'. I'd tried to make an effort with Caitlin. I tried to understand how hard it must be to see her father happy. I tried to recall too that the first time I'd seen Caitlin (from a distance and she hadn't spoken) I had somewhat of a girl crush on her. However, the 'little misunderstanding' three months ago really sealed our fate.

Caitlin had been stuck for someone to pick Joey up from Nursery. I volunteered. Not because I particularly wanted to spend time with my almost-step-grandson, but because I thought it might make her see that I wasn't the enemy. Maybe it would have done. If I hadn't picked up the wrong child. Oh, I know, classic sitcom moment. Turns out, it's not actually that funny. The Police turned up to remove the boy (a cool kid called Brandon) from my care. The man from Social Services was really pissed off. He'd planned a half day and 'cba' ('couldn't be arsed' - but as a trusted member of the council he wasn't allowed to say that in full so he was professional and used the abbreviation) dealing with 'inadequates who identified children by the little ducky trousers they're wearing'. In my defence Caitlin had said they were a 'one off'. Turns out Asda's finest.

That social worker used to come into the Centre. It was bloody embarrassing. Of course, my old Gran would have said 'you'll live a long time after you're embarrassed' but she didn't see Caitlin's face that night. 'Bloody incompetent', 'flighty' and, to Ron, 'your bloody midlife crisis' were some of the politer terms she used to describe me. Ron had spent the past few months trying to smooth it all over. Reasoning, 'tempers were flying high' and, far less convincingly, 'it could have happened to anyone'. Brandon, on the plus side, had a great day. I bought him an ice-cream and, until the whole handcuffing part, I was rocking the babysitting deal.

Yes, life had taught me a lot in the past year. Namely that fairy tales had it all wrong. It's not the evil stepmother you have to worry about. She gets a bad press. Fairy tales just short circuit to the ending. They don't tell you about the reasonable provocation that's gone before. When you're a stepmother you'll be cheering on the 'witch' when she hands that bitch Snow White the poisoned apple. Getting the Woodcutter to chop out her heart for good measure really was the only sensible solution. That's why fairy tales end with the wedding. If the cameras kept rolling, the harsh truth would unfold. The stepmother wasn't evil. Cinderella, Snow White and all the others. They had it coming.

CHAPTER 6

"Caitlin's having a hard time."

Because life is a Mardi Gras for me.

Ron nuzzled the back of my neck once we were safely at home. I tried not to notice he hid any physical contact from Caitlin. Or feel that sometimes I was like another child in the situation.

"Thank you for your patience." He put his arms around my waist as he flicked on the coffee maker. I could tell it was going to be another long night. Ron had waited patiently as Caitlin ordered green tea after green tea for what felt like an eternity. He nodded intently at her tales of car pools and agency nannies. He invited her back to the flat when it felt like she was going to take up residence in the restaurant she had her offspring had cleared. Thankfully, that brought the evening to an end. At least, the part of the evening she had featured in. There would be many hours ahead for Ron.

"Has Caitlin ever been to our flat?"

Ron sighed. "She's having a tough time. She's not always like that."

She had been since I'd known her.

I smiled as though I understood; as though I hadn't been considering how to have Caitlin adopted or, better yet, deported. I'd stopped saying that Caitlin didn't like me. There was no need to underline the obvious. Ron had given up protesting that 'she just needs to get to know you'. Once that happened Caitlin actively hated me. I knew Ron had a daughter. I understood she would be important in our lives. I just never thought it would feel like she was running them.

I was pleased to be back in our kitchen, in our little flat. I told myself the lighting in the restaurant was off. It was Caitlin's presence that dulled my sparkle and, yet, I still couldn't bring myself to even glance at a reflective surface. I didn't want to see the sadness again. I was worried it was still there. Worried that kind of sadness had to have been around for a while. It couldn't have arrived or gone so quickly. I was worried about what that meant.

Ron's eyes caught mine. Did he see it too? For a moment a silence stood between us and I was frightened about what he might say next. My stomach churned. Although that could have been the paneer. It's not supposed to be green, right? *Jen, focus.*

"Do you think we could have been exposed to noxious chemicals the night the Centre burnt down?"

I hadn't even been thinking that but some part of my brain needed an explanation for how I looked. Sick was better than sad.

"I doubt it." Ron considered the question seriously. "We were out in the fresh air and the Fire Brigade didn't ask us to move back."

Not until those teens brought the marshmallows to toast anyway.

"Are you feeling unwell?" He looked concerned.

"I'm ok." The hollow mantra of the past few weeks.

"Are you sure?"

I knew from the tone of his voice Ron needed me to be fine.

"I need to look at those papers." His tone was apologetic but concealing himself in the spare room was the new norm.

I wanted to tell him that I needed him here. That we needed to repair some of the emotional damage from his vicious offspring but, Ron had a proper grown-up job and there was a proper grown-up big deal/event/meeting looming.

I nodded to demonstrate agreement, understanding or just acceptance. I pretended I'd been hanging on his every word on the four thousand other occasions he'd spoken about it. What really happens is that little circus song plays in my head and a hamster starts to juggle. I wasn't interested in finance when I worked for Ron. I was less interested now he'd stopped paying me - for work I mean. It would be weird if he ever paid me for sex. Mum wouldn't have liked that either: too reminiscent of cousin Lyz.

"I'm pretty exhausted." I tried to sound bright and cheerful. Too bright and chipper for someone claiming to be exhausted. "I think I'll have an early night."

"In that case…." Ron pulled me closer.

It was refreshing to see he could still be playful; that he still found me attractive.

"You get back to those papers." I tried to sound convincing. "You need to prepare." For whatever is happening tomorrow. That had been the plan for this evening. Until summoned by Her Majesty. I bloody hated her but even I had to admit it's not like she'd ruined our evening. Ron would have banished himself to the office earlier. I would have been hauled up watching whatever was trending on Netflix. Alone. I never noticed I was lonely when I had to work in the evening too. No, not lonely. *Stop it. Ron and I are happy. It's Caitlin that's the problem. Caitlin's the bitch.*

Ron frowned. He'd been doing that a lot lately. Usually after we met with Caitlin and now, increasingly, before. He was quieter too. Gone were the reassurances that she'd 'come around'. This was going to be our lives together and I was beginning to wonder if that would be enough. I loved Ron. I loved Ron to the point of distraction. We'd been together for eight months and in all that time were inseparable. Ron lived in my flat (the new one, the one he hadn't repossessed); which is a bit odd as it's much smaller than his. Ron's flat is closer to where we both work and he has parking. Yet, my flat had become ours. Something I'd told myself would never

49

happen again. We were supposed to buy somewhere to be 'ours' but, I'd never afford my half of the mortgage. Besides, I'd lost everything in my last relationship, including myself. So, for now, it suited me to stay here. To tell myself if this relationship didn't work out I'd only loose him. I'd pretend that thought was bearable.

We're happy. In this little flat. In this little bubble. We love each other unconditionally and without limit. Caitlin's just a smack in the face. A potent reminder that our relationship causes Ron pain.

I pretended not to watch as Ron hugged and kissed Caitlin and Joey before they got into the taxi. I nodded, coldly, as Caitlin made eye contact over her father's shoulder. He noticed too that, although she held him in an embrace, it was forced and distant. I was driving a wedge between Ron and his daughter. I hadn't really seen it until tonight. Until tonight I thought it was just me she hated.

CHAPTER 7

"You're quiet." Ron was standing at the bedroom door drinking his morning coffee.

I'd pretended to be asleep when he finally came to be bed last night and I'd got up really early for a 'run'. I'd downloaded the *Couch to 5k* App last week and really nailed the couch part. I ended up at the newsagent on the corner of the road. Then the park to tuck into my bar of whole nut chocolate and read the latest trashy magazine. I wanted to feel guilty about my lack of purpose and drive but I'd read a text from Ron's personal trainer saying he'd missed the past three sessions. In Ron's case he'd be working but, still, it showed an apathy to personal fitness I could really get on board with. However, unlike me, Ron was still in tremendous shape. He remained athletic, and much as Caitlin liked to make a thing of the age difference, when we were together, when it was just us, we didn't feel generations apart. Ron didn't just look good for a man of his age, he looked good. When people assume that I'm his daughter now it's because they think he could do better.

"I'm not feeling too good." That much was true. I felt sick. It was a family-sized bar of chocolate and I ate it surprisingly quickly. Maybe I'd given myself diabetes. Managing that could keep me occupied. I could do with a hobby now that I was unemployed. Maybe something a bit better than a life changing medical condition though.

I hadn't slept well either. I knew what lay ahead. I saw it in Ron's eyes when Caitlin awkwardly hugged her father and jumped in the taxi.

"I'm just going back to bed for a bit." I knew going back to bed was the wrong thing to do. The tiredness was apathy and laying around all day wasn't going to give me any more purpose or energy.

Caitlin's passive aggressive campaign was getting harder and harder to bounce back from. She could do it now with a look. A comment about her mother and a glance that said to me: 'You're only sitting here because she isn't.' Caitlin's a potent reminder of Ron's life before. An entire lifetime pulling us apart. That's why we stayed here. Ron's flat belonged to Laura.

No, Jen. Stop. You're spiralling. This is just how Caitlin wants you to feel. Only...

It wasn't just Caitlin.

I didn't cope well without a job. Without focus. When Stephen left me high and dry, the first thing I did was went to the Job Centre. Ron dashing off to work all stressed out made me feel increasingly useless and guilty. The most stressful thing I'd encounter all day would be *Bargain Hunt*. I'd briefly considered a career in antique dealing. I thought I had all this innate knowledge about how much cameo brooches retailed for at auction. Turns out I'd just seen that episode before. Several times. I was a day-time TV zombie. Little wonder I bored Ron. I bored myself.

Ron stood between me and the door. "Are you sure you're ok?"

He felt my forehead like any good parent. I'll be offered some Calpol next.

Ron's question felt like a trap. As though he wanted me to open up the discussion that would shut our relationship down.

"You were late to bed last night." I skirted around the edges of some of the issues. I should have added, 'again'.

"I'm sorry." Ron leaned his head against mine. It was the gesture that brought time to a standstill. It silenced all the other noise in my head.

Perhaps it would be easier just to begin the ending of all of this now.

"I think I've just got the unemployment blues."

I knew it wasn't the right moment but that felt like a catchy song title. I wondered if Neil could play the guitar.

"I could work at home if you like." Ron put his arm around me and for a moment I allowed myself to feel safe, cocooned from the world outside. From Caitlin.

I tried to feel that Ron's presence here would be a comfort; that, this time, he was offering his company too. I knew better. If Ron stayed at home he would be locked away in the study.

"I'll be fine." My voice cracked.

"I love you, Jen. Nothing and no one will ever come between us. I promise."

Bless him. He really meant it but, those promises can't be made. If it was a competition between me and his daughter- I didn't want to win.

"Now," he smiled. "Are you sure you don't want me to come back to bed?"

CHAPTER 8

By Monday morning I was feeling much more optimistic. Sunday night had been 'Netflix and chill'. A phrase I'm really hoping my mother will stop using when she finds out what it means.

Ron had taken time off from the dreaded papers. Not because they were no longer important but because our relationship was important too. He glanced anxiously towards the study door a few times but bravely fought the call of the spreadsheet. We both felt the benefit of it. I bounced out of bed more determined than ever to get life back on track. I could make Caitlin like me. I could make anyone like me. Look at Neil, when he was signed off sick (at the Job Centre) the doctor gave me a name check in his sick note. Now we're, well not friends exactly, but we don't hate each other. It could be done.

"You're late." Neil tapped his watch. Pointless. He wasn't my boss and he'd dropped that watch in the bath last week. The screen had gone all blurry. He kept it, a relic of 'him': the mystery man. It looked expensive.

"And you look like shit." Neil's latest therapist told him he bottled things up too much and part of 'healing'

55

was to say whatever was on his mind. We'd been having a lot of 'truth bombs'. He'd been punched twice already this month.

"I don't work here anymore. I've been paid off." Chris clearly hadn't breached confidentiality and told Neil he was now the sole employee of the burnt out shell.

"Really?" Neil's voice cracked with emotion and for a second I thought he might cry.

"Better me than you." I jumped to his defence. "Like Chris said, I don't really need to work." He might have had a different view had I shown him the hairy arm charts.

"Have the Fire Brigade cleared it for us to be here?" Parts of the building had literally imploded in the flames.

"There's little structural damage to the office." Neil spoke with confidence. I wondered if any of the fire fighters had followed up on his offer of a curry. I wondered how the mystery man felt if they had.

"The office is part of the older building." It sounded as though Neil was quoting a report.

The swanky new part of the Centre had been added at the renovation.

"They used to build things to last." I agreed.

Perhaps it was part of some new council initiative; use Amazon boxes as construction materials. It felt like the extension had been specifically built just to burn.

"What are you doing?"

Neil appeared to be sifting through the remnants of the office. In truth, I had come here to be alone.

The fire was almost a month ago but everything was still cold and damp. "People say it's the water that does the real damage but you never quite believe it."

Neil looked around the mush. "The mould will set in soon."

"It's so bloody depressing."

"Really, this is exactly how I thought all this would end." There was a small hint of a smile as he said it.

"Just another Monday." He mocked.

Neil was supposed to have been at the Centre today for the planned 'income maximisation event' where we ensure families are receiving all the supports they're entitled to. 'Other than actually getting a job,' Caitlin had quipped. I mean honestly, do I want someone like that to like me? It's impossible to believe that Ron's her father. He did say he hadn't been a 'hands-on parent'. Who could blame him? He'd have had his hands around her neck within minutes.

'People like that need understanding.' Neil had tried to calm me one morning as I'd been full on ranting about Caitlin. Neil was wrong. People like Caitlin need to be left in the wilderness.

"So, why are you here?" He threw a soggy packet of cookies in the bin. "You don't even come to work when you're supposed to."

"I come." I protested. "Eventually."

I had nowhere else to go. Ron looked stressed again and this whole Caitlin thing had thrown me. I constantly felt just a tiny bit squeamish that all this happiness could suddenly just end. Impending doom, like the sword of Damocles just about to fall. Why can't I say clever things like that out loud? I'll try and work that into the conversation.

"Hey Neil, do you ever feel like…"

He looked up, tired and broken. Neil had been on the steady decline for weeks but I'd been too wrapped up in my own drama to notice.

"I didn't feel too good and wanted to get out the house."

Germ-phobic Neil recoiled in horror.

"I think it's just food poisoning."

His eyes glazed over. He was expecting a segway into the C-bomb and a detailed account of the disastrous weekend 'family meal'. It had become our regular Monday meeting item.

I looked around the shell of the Centre. What I really wanted to do was tell him about the hat. Caitlin sitting, surrounded by ferns, looking like Indiana Jones or that guy from Breaking Bad was an image we would have laughed about a few months ago. One of us would have bought a hat from a joke shop and we would have taken turns to play the petulant Caitlin. A few months ago none of this would have felt so insurmountable.

"I'm assuming we're closed." *We.* This place was no longer me.

Neil looked embarrassed. "Coronary Chris wants me to keep an eye on the place."

"He's promoted you?" I tried not to feel resentment that the greatest snowflake of our generation had been given this responsibility over me. Not that there was much left to be responsible for. At least now Neil had a clear job description.

"They can't just get rid of me, Jen. I've been employed by the Council for years. They'll have to pay me anyway. I'm a glorified caretaker. Not that there's much left to care for."

I shouldn't have come here. Or maybe that was why I had come. I had to see again how fragile success was. How quickly it could all be taken away.

"Why wasn't Chris here the night of the fire?" Moaning about Chris could pull us back together. Maybe it was the Centre being gone, my obsession with Caitlin or my recent unemployment but I felt real distance between Neil and I. I didn't like it.

Neil shrugged. Unwilling to be drawn on another one of our favourite topics.

"Probably in some kind of medically induced coma. I suppose the real question is how is that man still alive?" His voice full of bitterness and resentment.

I couldn't ask Neil if he was ok. Not again. It was perfectly clear he wasn't going to talk about the mystery man. As Neil sifted through the debris I felt a pang. He didn't want to talk to me about anything. This another place I was unwanted.

Neil looked up, briefly. He saw the sadness and misinterpreted it as related to our work situation.

"I thought you said that all endings were a new beginning."

I said lots of things. "Are you sure that was me?"

It could have been during my inspirational calendar phase. Actually, I think Neil had given me that. Back in the day when he burned with enthusiasm for his new leading man. Neil was full of pithy phrases that felt reassuring but meant nothing. I was going to hook Neil and Mum up on social media. Then, I thought between them they'd probably inadvertently start some kind of cult.

Neil had looked brighter then too. The blond tips in his hair were a bold 'fashion' choice that he had stood by for several months. They'd grown out now. He hadn't even bothered to have the ends cut away. A patchy beard spread haphazardly over his face too. Less of a fashion choice and more something that just happened. A physical reminder that self-care was just out of reach.

"I'm sorry," I whispered. Realising, only now, I'd let the world burn around me.

"I'm so sorry I've been preoccupied." Maybe it was too late to reach out. Maybe the void between us was too great.

Neil looked at me again. I could see his defences weaken. "You really do look like shit."

I felt like it too.

'That's just the demon hormones.' Ron had assured me this morning before he kissed me passionately, demonstrating that he still found me attractive as I

60

struggled to get into my skinny jeans. Ron wanted me even without make-up, even before I'd brushed my teeth. He understood the demon hormones and the lies they told me each month. 'You're too fat,' was their go-to complaint. Only this time my clothes, mirrors and scales were in on it too.

'It's your fault,' I pretended to protest. 'Happiness makes me fat.' Ron smiled again. 'Well, maybe we have time to burn a few calories.'

I loved those moments. When I felt him drifting back. When it felt like us as we'd always been - honest, uncomplicated, happy.

Ron made mountains into molehills. Problems shared with him dissipated. I couldn't give up on us so easily. I'd win Caitlin over. I had to.

Neil looked at me suspiciously. "You haven't been feeling well for a few weeks. Do you think the evil step-daughter is trying to poison you?"

It had crossed my mind.

CHAPTER 9

Carol looked away as I stuck a chip in my Cream Egg McFlurry.

"When you said we should meet for lunch I had higher hopes." She tried to hide the disdain in her voice.

"I'm unemployed."

"I'm not. I could have sprung for lunch."

"I don't need you to pay for lunch." I heard the defensiveness in my tone.

The place was packed with rowdy teens. The very fact I had described them as that made me feel older and less like myself.

Chris was on his way to the Centre again. Neil had tried to be polite but had essentially told me to piss off before he arrived.

"I've been feeling unwell." Is that what was wrong with me?

Carol raised an eyebrow.

"I thought this would help." I couldn't tell her that I didn't want to be alone. That, for a few minutes, I just wanted to feel like me. Only now, McDonald's on a bank holiday Monday didn't really feel like me either.

"I worry about your instincts, Jen. This food is a cure for nothing." Carol pushed her burger away. Probably wise.

"Haven't your heard of the viral migraine hack?" I tried to defend my choice. Perhaps that was another one of my faults; never admitting when I was wrong.

"The migraine hack is triptans and you won't get them here." Carol watched as a hooded youth sat down at the table opposite. "I take that back."

I wanted to tell Carol she shouldn't judge by appearance but, if I had to draw a drug dealer, the guy opposite is pretty much what I'd draw.

My cousin Carol got all the good genes in our family. She was strong, confident and successful. They'd just used what was left to make me. Carol had her life together. She had been married to Alice for longer than I can remember. Carol even had a hobby (although please don't tell her I called it that as, for her, 'blogging is my one true passion'). Full disclosure, I'm not entirely sure I understand what a blog is. I don't think anyone does. I try to show an interest but that hamster starts juggling.

"We used to come here all the time." I thought of thirteen-year-old Carol excitedly collecting her Happy Meal and diving into the box for the toy.

"We came here twice." Carol took antibacterial spray from her bag and used a napkin to clean the table. It was hard to believe that Carol had ever been a child. Or, that she had ever been excited about anything. She was so composed now. Always acting with dignity.

Two teenagers started throwing fries at each other.

"Life was simpler back then."

"Was it?" Carol frowned.

I was pleased to see her brows furrow. Mum was obsessed that Carol and Alice had Botox parties every other week. It seemed unlikely but, I knew I would have to talk to her about it at some point. Somewhere along the line Carol and I had moved from cousins to wellbeing monitors.

"You didn't worry about cleaning tables." I tried to present the evidence.

"You didn't worry about landfill and climate change."

True. I too had been excited about the plastic tat.

Carol put the spray back in her bag. "I had other worries back then. Like my parents' divorce, my sexuality." She folded her arms impatient again. "Jen, what is this about?"

"I just thought it would be nice to meet."

"I can think of nicer places. When people start looking back it's usually a sign of anxiety."

"Who said I'm anxious? You're the one doing the Howard Hughes with the tables." If we weren't careful we'd be heading into a full on bicker.

"Howard Hughes wasn't cleaning OCD. He kept jars of urine and used tissues."

"Good to know." Although it wasn't helping me feel less nauseous.

"People look back when they are anxious because the past feels safer." Carol frustratingly levelled her tone.

Perhaps all I needed to feel better was a good argument.

"We know how our worries turned out. Mum and Dad remarried, everyone loves Alice." Carol held up her hand, as though she had conclusively proved her point. Yet, the conviction that 'everyone loved Alice' had sounded hollow. So hollow I didn't even need to point out the statement was untrue. I didn't dislike Alice. Worse. I had no real opinion of her.

"Today I have different worries." Carol continued.

I wondered if her marriage was one of them.

"Like what?"

"Like why my deranged cousin wanted to come to McDonalds."

"Being deranged isn't a good enough explanation?" I allowed a smile.

For years Carol and I hadn't been close. Then, one day, when my life spectacularly fell to crap, Carol kicked my butt until I sorted it all out. I owed Carol a lot. Maybe I should have splashed out on Pizza Hut.

"It's complicated." I offered. It's wasn't. It never is. All that little soundbite means is I'm tolerating the intolerable and I can't even articulate why.

"Jen, I have about a million meetings this afternoon."

"That seems hyperbole." I was trying a new word a day online calendar. I was glad I had managed to work in yesterday's word to today's conversation.

Full disclosure, I've no idea what Carol does. She seems to be really good at it and it appears to pay well but, honestly, not a clue. She works in a shiny glass building. A bit like Ron's. I'd no real idea what he does either and not only do we live together but, I worked for him.

"If you need to get back." I heard the hollowness of my voice. I felt it too.

"That's not what I meant." Carol leaned forward. "Just, if you are going to sit here and lie to yourself it seems you can do that without having me around."

Ok, Jen. Deep breaths. "Maybe, I'm looking back because I feel like there's nothing to look forward too." Like all the best days have already been.

"You know that's not true."

Carol was much more patient when you lowered the mask and just told the truth.

"And ...." I took a deep breath because I could tell Carol. I could tell her anything. "There's no mirrors here."

"What?" Carol looked around the glass building. "Jen," she lowered her voice. "You're not taking cocaine are you? Is that why you're so down."

"No, I'm not taking bloody cocaine. Might be an idea. It might perk me up."

Carol looked dubious. "I don't think it would work that way with you."

I wondered what she was implying. I could research it later online. I had nothing else to do.

"Why are you concerned about the presence of mirrors?" Carol leaned back in her chair, exasperated. "You've not been dabbling in the occult again."

It was one time.

"I don't want to see my reflection. I look so sad." The windows here had a persistent greasy film. They reflected nothing but distorted shapes.

I thought Carol would laugh. I thought she would dismiss it or tell me to pull myself together but she didn't. Carol reached out and took my hand and, for the first time in her life, she said, nothing.

CHAPTER 10

"Why do you think Neil is being so secretive about this new guy?"

Two teenagers in the corner were bringing a new meaning to public display of affection. It was sort of repulsive but, kind of inspiring too. Their relationship looked so uncomplicated.

Carol shrugged. "Why do you care?"

She'd had the same assistant for four years and still isn't entirely sure of her name. 'Amy or Angela', she'd guessed the last time I'd asked. Carol is not what you'd call a 'people person'.

"I don't care really." But I did.

"Neil usually tells me everything." I mean, too much. The man has no filter.

"Except with this guy. Nothing has slipped."

"Jen." Carol's tone was firm. "You said you looked sad. Do you have any thoughts on why that could be?"

"My friends don't trust me." I stirred the melted ice-cream. I hadn't even managed to eat that in the end.

"What is it that you notice about yourself." Carol tried a different tactic. "What don't you like about your reflection?"

"It doesn't look like me."

The person who stared back at me was often quiet and still. Not in the calm, composed, collected way of Carol but as withdrawn, hunched and broken. It was the reflection of a person just fading away. A person who was trying desperately not to be seen.

"Caitlin hates me and, try as I might, I can't change that." The words came from what was left of my soul.

"Yeah, well," Carol pulled out her blackberry distractedly, "she has met you." Carol gave a wry little smile.

I've never had a blackberry. My input to any work environment has never been so crucial that I needed to be 'online even when I'm offline'. When the Centre burned down I suggested to Ron I come back to the office to help relieve the burden (whatever that was). He'd laughed for a full ten minutes. I'd sort of been joking, but it's still quite offensive.

"And you lost her baby." Caitlin began to scroll through her emails.

"I didn't *lose* him. I just took the wrong one. Anyway, Brandon's Mum was cool with it." We still grab a coffee. I just didn't mention to the vegan Linda I'd bought her son an ice-cream. I'd checked with the woman behind the counter that kids can have ice-cream. It could have been like puppies; you think you're being kind and suddenly you've killed them. From the look that vendor gave me I would put money on it being her who called the Police.

"Who's Brandon?"

"What do you think I should do?" I needed Carol to remain focused. One of us had to. We'd passed a fish tank in a shop window on the way here. One lone fish. It looked depressed. Maybe I should get a fish. That fish. I could liberate it in a poorly conceived heist.

"Do you think I should get a fish?"

Carol put her phone down on the table. "I don't know Jen. It's been six months and by the sound of it Caitlin hates you more than ever."

I hadn't even told her about Saturday night.

"I've read her social media posts."

Great, I'd gone viral and not in a good way. Never in a good way.

Maybe this crappy feeling was just a virus. My stomach churned. The ice-cream and chips that had soothed any woe as a child tasted like chalk. Only, if this was a virus it had been going on for weeks.

"Why do you care if Caitlin hates you?"

"I care what people think. Unlike you."

"No, you don't." Carol glanced around to check no one was listening. "It's one of the things I respect about you."

I grabbed my phone and pretended to record a voice note. "Say that again."

"Say what again?" She looked away.

"One of the things you respect about me?"

"Don't get excited." Carol checked her watch. "It's not a long list."

"She's Ron's daughter."

"That's why he can't say she's a bitch." Carol dismissed.

"He doesn't even seem to think it."

"Sure he does. He must. Parents aren't blind to their children's faults. They just try to ignore them."

"Things are different with Ron." I ventured.

"You're living together. That changes a relationship. When Alice and I first moved in together …." She trailed off. Carol spoke very little about her relationship with Alice.

I waited. I hoped that Carol would say more.

She didn't.

"Is that why you rarely speak about Alice? It was so hard for you to be together that you don't want to say anything negative?"

"Don't start getting all insightful." Carol mocked. "I'm just a private person."

About some things. I was fully briefed on Carol's perimenopause.

She grabbed a chip and dipped it in the melted ice-cream. Her mellowing made us both smile.   "He's sick of me." I glanced briefly to check for a reaction. Nothing.

"I can't focus. You know what my mind is like. Racing from one thing to another. It's exhausting for me. How must it be for Ron?"

Carol sat quietly. Her stillness was unsettling.

"It's not that you can't focus, Jen. It's that you're interested in so many things at once."

"Same thing." It was moments like this I knew that Carol loved me. When she tried to protect my feelings about the things I couldn't change.

"No, it's not. You see what other people don't. Right now you are taking in aspects of this environment I haven't even noticed. So, yeah. I get that can be overwhelming. You just need a bit more time to filter out what is unimportant."

Like the noise of the teenagers, the smell of bleach and the scraping of chairs.

"Caitlin's not just background noise. She's Ron's daughter and if it comes to a choice …." I could feel the tears stinging my eyes. I couldn't finish the thought never mind the sentence.

"It's not going to come to that." Carol pushed her 'tap water' aside. Wise again. It looked grey.

I wanted to agree. I wanted to be as sure as Ron had sounded when he said nothing would come between us, but things were changing. He puts his phone away or closes his laptop when I come into the room. There's something he doesn't want me to see. It's not that I don't trust him but, when I checked the internet history it had been deleted. Maybe he was looking at Caitlin's social media too. Finding out how much his daughter hated me this week. He probably charts it in a graph.

"He's a bit distant. At times." I hadn't meant to say it. The world was supposed to think Ron and I were the perfect couple. Saying it out loud made it real. Like, maybe it wasn't the fish that was lonely. Maybe it was me.

Stop it, Jen. Remember, you are happy.

Only, you shouldn't have to remind yourself that you're happy.

"There's a lot going on at Smiths." Carol trotted out the trusted phrase.

I nodded knowingly and prepared the hamster to juggle.

"And, do these quiet times coincide with you plaguing him with questions?" Carol sounded increasingly impatient.

"Like what?" I snipped.

"Like whether octopuses have knees."

Sometimes.

CHAPTER 11

Ron texted asking me to meet him for lunch. With all the extra time on my hands I was feeling too available. In many ways it was a lot like being back at Smiths. I often dropped everything to do as I pleased. Sometimes literally. I broke three laptops that way.

I contemplated giving Ron a bit of a run around. Caitlin always did. Whenever Ron suggests meeting up she usually has something planned. Or, she usually has something planned when I was involved.

"Why are we in a bathroom fixtures and fittings shop?"

Ron had been very urgent in his request. Time and location all communicated in a perfectly punctuated text. I deliberately texted back, 'K'. Maybe our relationship wasn't lovely. Maybe we were in a rut. A new bathroom would be unlikely to help. I had always fancied one of those bath tubs with the gold feet though. We could put it in the spare room/cupboard under the futon.

"I thought it was romantic." Ron's eyes twinkled. I was relieved to see him happy, or drunk. Either way I decided not to ask him what the 'lot going on at Smiths was.

"This place is literally called 'Pulling the Plug'."

Maybe this was it. The 'we need some time apart' talk. Ron had chosen somewhere I'd never go. He was thoughtful like that. He wouldn't want me to pass this place and remember this is where we called it a day. Ron looked relieved because you always are, aren't you? Once you've made the life changing decision.

It was good that he had kept his flat. I understood now why it had lain empty for the past six months. Insurance. Ron had needed a way out.

He smiled and pulled me into a shower cubicle.

"If this is your idea of romance Mr. Smith then you're really phoning it in." I tried to sound casual. As though the world was not about to end, again.

He leaned in closer. "You really don't remember where you are?"

Great, now the Alzheimer's had kicked in.

"This is where we had our first date. At Hype."

"It wasn't a date." I smiled. The first real smile in weeks. "You were my boss. I probably should have gone to HR."

I had many encounters with HR. David and Janice told me my antics had made into office folklore and the employee handbook now had three updated sections because of me.

Ron was right about our location. The trendy restaurant that looked set to conquer the world for at least two weeks, replaced by a coffee shop, then a laundrette and now, this.

"This," Ron leaned in closer, "is almost the exact spot our table was that night." He beamed triumphantly. "Now, tell me that's not romantic."

"Or some form of autism. It's a thin line." I leaned in closer too. Hoping we could stay in this place together, forever.

"I know things have been increasingly stressful and weird with …." He paused. Avoiding conjuring she who should not be named. In a shop surrounded by mirrors I was wary too. I heard if you say her name three times it opens the gates of Hell.

"Everything." I offered with a conspiratorial smile.

Ron placed his forehead against mine. "She warms up."

I resented in this perfect moment her malevolent name still hung in the air between us.

"This is just a little bump in the road." He placed his arms around my waist.

"Don't push me away." His vulnerable plead hurt.

Ron had felt the distance too.

"Like Saturday night." I whispered.

"Like Saturday night." He agreed; serious again. Although he had been the one disappearing into the office to look at 'papers'. I decided not to bring that up either. I regretted having to let so much slide to maintain the moment.

"I'm sorry." I'd let Ron merge into Caitlin and felt resentment towards them both. I hated Caitlin for how she treated me but resented too that Ron let her.

"Don't be sorry. Just tell me what you're thinking."

Ron didn't want to know what I was thinking. I wanted this relationship to work. I mean none of the others had but, what the hell. On reflection some of those relationships failed because I told people what I was thinking, like, 'Do you ever think 'What if I just kicked that toddler?'' Then, there were the things I thought but didn't say. Like, 'I'm worried I've invested everything in this'. When Stephen left it destroyed me financially and it almost emotionally broke me. I swore I'd never love anyone again but when I met Ron I realised what love really meant. Ron didn't want to hear what I thought of his daughter. I didn't like Caitlin. I'd never like Caitlin. I was finding it increasingly hard just to tolerate her. The truth would devastate him and tear us apart.

"What if being with me drives a wedge between you?" I hadn't meant to speak. My role in these conversations was simply to smile and bravely nod.

Caitlin was the only issue we danced around. Honestly, last month I had terrible stomach flu and Ron sat with me, in the bathroom, as I recreated the iconic vomiting scene from *The Exorcist*. I thought we could conquer anything. Then I met her. Talking about Caitlin would only bring the end quicker.

"Eventually Caitlin will see what the rest of the world does. How happy you make me. Then she'll get over it."

"What if the bump never goes away?"

Stop talking Jen. You don't want this to be the place where it began and ended.

"Then we'll live with it." Ron took my hand and kissed it. "Together."

He pulled me closer. Telling me to talk and then distracting me with the laws of attraction.

"And who could fail to love you? I promise you," he kissed me gently, "all of this is just footnotes."

My stomach lurched. Footnotes and small print had burst our bubble once before.

CHAPTER 12

Mum laughed. "He really knows you!"

The Bathroom Showroom incident had really tickled her. More so when it concluded with us being asked to leave by the manager. She didn't share my righteous indignation that the staff at 'Pulling the Plug' thought I was a prostitute. She just looked over her reading glasses. 'Were you wearing that top?'

It was hard to be optimistic about life when even your fat jeans don't fit but one of the positive aspects of weight gain was a pretty impressive cleavage.

"Do you notice anything different?" Mum looked eagerly around the room. Those kind of questions always felt like a trap.

"I like your hair." That sounded like a question.

"We painted the kitchen!" She rolled her eyes, dramatically.

"It's always been green."

"It's two shades lighter." Mum smirked, as though I was being the unreasonable one.

That's the thing with retirement. A few more weeks of unemployment and I'll have memorised the Dulux colour chart too. This was my third coffee stop of the day.

I was relieved to be back in my childhood home. Relieved and anxious. I couldn't see Ron and I in this kind of domestic bliss. I'd suggested painting our bedroom last week and he barely looked up from his phone. 'Hm' was as much enthusiasm as he could muster. Ron and I wouldn't be painting walls together. He'd get someone else in to do it. Maybe Chris was right. Maybe Ron and I were in different places in our lives.

"Do you need a hand with anything?" Maybe I had too much time on my hands. Too much time to think and amplify all my problems. Sometimes solutions come when we aren't looking for them. I think that was on the calendar Neil had bought for the office.

"Like what?" Mum looked confused.

"Decorating."

Her face changed to horror. Any task would go smoother without my involvement. "Are you OK, love?"

"Footnotes." My heart had pounded since Ron said it. An anxious knot had taken hold in my stomach.

"Remember, I found out in the footnotes that Smiths had underwritten my business loan, foreclosed and took my flat. If I had read the footnotes."

"It was a turn of phrase, love." Mum dismissed. "That's all in the past. Ron wasn't to blame. It was that…"

Mum still wouldn't say Stephen's name. It was now synonymous with an expanding range of expletives. I wondered if Ron's name would be eradicated from history too.

"His daughter hates me." I heard the crack in my voice as I felt like I was about to repeat the conversation with Carol. It is easy to lie to the world. Not so to your own mother.

"So what? She's the same age as you."

"Exactly!" Although there was a few years difference Caitlin and I probably could be described as the same generation.

"I just meant she's never going to pick your nursing home. Besides, I follow that one on the socials and she hates everyone."

Mum's use of social media worried me.

"I don't want him to have to choose."

I wondered what I expected Mum to say. What it was that I needed to hear to end the cycle.

"That's not going to happen. He's never going to let that happen. You two are destined to be together. It's Besheven." Mum beamed. "That's Yiddish for meant to be."

"Mum, we're not Jewish." The new neighbours four doors down were. Since Mum retired she's burned through a series of hobbies and interests. Religion seemed to be the latest fascination. Mum decided, this week anyway, that Judaism was her chosen pathway. She'd been a Ba'hai for three weeks last month. I'd contemplated buying her a dog.

"What if she hates me forever?"

Mum shrugged. "Let her."

I couldn't. It would destroy Ron. Slowly, over time, it would destroy us too. Ron understood that. I read it in his face most days.

"What if you hooked up with someone I hated? Would you dump them?"

"No." Mum looked thoughtfully at her coffee. "But, I suspect your father might make me. He's unreasonable like that."

Mum and Dad had been married forever. I should listen to their advice. They're almost the same generation as Ron too.

Don't say it. You don't want to say it. Once you say it you can never take it back.

"Do you think Ron's too old?" It felt like time stopped. As though the rest of my existence dependence on her answer. I had to fill the silence.

"I mean, do you think he is too old for me?"

Mum paused. She put her coffee down on the table and held my gaze. "When I first met him, I don't know. I was surprised. Maybe, I thought you relationship with Ron was a reaction to that codswalloper."

I wasn't even sure that was a word.

"But what I saw before I even met Ron was how happy he made you. From the moment you met him there was something different about you. That ….," she took a deep breath. "That last relationship. " She said the word with much disdain. " He was the same age as you. Way before that shitbag did what he did he stole your sparkle."

It felt like I had little left of that now.

"With Ron, there's so much more to your relationship than age." Mum held my hand. "He gets you, Jen. He really does."

He used to.

"I suppose I'm just feeling…" I trailed off. I hoped that Mum would have told me how it was that I was feeling. Perhaps if I could name it I could begin to address it.

"I feel like I've lost a bit of my sparkle." Was all I could muster. Perhaps this is just what it is like to finally grow-up.

"There's a lot going on, love." Was all Mum would commit to. Not quite agreement but not open descent.

I smiled and pretended as though it had been a fleeting thought. As though it had only occurred to me because of Caitlin.

"She's invited me for birthday drinks." Through Ron. Not directly. I expected he'd practically told Caitlin I'd be coming. He thinks it's progress. I think it's a set up. Entrapment. Caitlin would have a hidden agenda. Ron was probably paying for the whole thing as a sweetener for my presence. I tried not to think about it. I kept having visions of me standing on a stage covered in pig's blood and that was the best case scenario.

Mum stirred her coffee thoughtfully. "Have you thought about what you might buy her?"

Caitlin's the kind of person who could be bought.

"I thought maybe I'd give her twenty pieces of silver so she could buy her soul back from the Devil."

Mum smirked, but she tried to hide it.

"I'll ask Ron."

She laughed. "Imagine the treasure you'd have had over the years if I'd consulted with your father."

Dad's gifts were legendary. He bought Mum a toaster for Valentine's Day this year and that was one of his better gifts.

"I did just have a date with Ron in a shower cubicle." Maybe my quirkiness was rubbing off on him.

A thoughtful gift could help steady the water. Like, I don't know, a goat for her voodoo witch sacrifices.

CHAPTER 13

"Chris has been on the phone again." I broke the bad news to Neil as soon as he appeared.

"You must feel violated." Neil placed the take away coffee down on the warped desk. The wood still hadn't completely dried. "All that heavy breathing are you sure it was Chris. Might just have been the local pervert."

"He was pissed off that I was here again."

Neil shrugged. "I'm pissed off the bloody phone still works."

Neil had to 'pop out' and reluctantly left me 'in charge'. He was lucky I'd decided to come back to the Community Centre. To be honest he probably expected it. I had been here every day this week with increasingly ridiculous excuses. 'Just passing by' was probably one of the weakest; this place wasn't on the way to anywhere. That was the first of its many problems. Poor location. Few travel links. You'd have thought the Council would have spotted that fatal flaw.

I suspected Neil had another tryst with the Mystery Man. I wanted to follow him. I was glad I didn't when he returned looking more annoyed than before.

"Crap." Neil slammed the coffees down on my water-damaged desk and threw some papers on the floor. "He's going to bloody 'pop in' again later."

Neil had said "bloody". Right in front of his fire-damaged swear jar.

I was the one who should have been narked. Neil could have been at the Job Centre finding me gainful employment. Or, in the Chapel praying to St. Jude (Patron Saint of Lost Causes). Someone had to take up my case.

"That's ok. I have stuff to do." I didn't but I couldn't be here when Chris made an appearance. My on-the-job philosophy had reverted to type. Be very half-assed at whatever you do so you aren't asked again. That's why Mum and Dad encouraged me to come and visit Neil today when I could have been helping them strip the wallpaper in the hallway. Chris visit could push my philosophy to the limit. You can't really take that half assed approach with CPR. Well, you probably shouldn't.

"I only really came to collect my stuff." I held up my partially melted *Frozen* pencil case. Elsa looked as though she'd stroked out. I'd amassed more but all the chocolate had melted then, been waterlogged and now, without heating, I suspect had solidified again

"Where did you have to dash off to so urgently?" I had told myself I wasn't going to ask. Only, it should have been obvious to Neil that I needed to live vicariously through others. He was just being spiteful in withholding information.

"Chris is always hanging around." Neil sulked and ignored the question. "I don't even know why they put me in charge of this."

I still wasn't sure what they'd put Neil in charge of. I'd spend quite a few days hanging around here and all we did was drink coffee. In some ways very little had changed. Only, I wasn't getting paid. That changed a power dynamic in a relationship. Especially when your partner already made so much more money than you.

Stop, this isn't about you're failing relationship. Look at Neil. Listen to what he's telling you. Or, more importantly, what he's not.

Neil heard my question. I saw that he heard it. I should respect his privacy and the professional boundary.

"You haven't knocked up this mystery bloke?" I tried to sound light-hearted. Like I wasn't massively pissed off he was constantly evasive. It wouldn't even be that interesting.

So why isn't he telling you?

"I don't have time for this. If Chris finds you here …." Neither of us was sure what he'd do. Chris hated me but I was connected to Ron and he's influential. Ron's my get out of jail free card.

Neil looked anxious. I wondered if he was still taking his medication. After 'the incident' the doctor thought it might calm his nerves. They offered it to a few other people who witnessed it. They all needed to be calmed down too.

I wasn't going to ask. Anxious people hate being asked.

"Are you still taking the tablets?" It's like my brain has no control over my mouth.

"I'm just a bit stressed," he snipped. "I'm allowed to be stressed."

"Yeah." I agreed. But Neil never gave a crap about the Centre. "What are you stressed about?"

"Why is Chris still hanging around? Isn't he like one of the big bosses?" Perhaps Neil tried to move us back to safer ground. The common enemy, hatred of authority and all that.

"Is that another dig about his weight?"

Chris had more than enough personality flaws for me to be concerned about his physical appearance.

"He's more of an advert for the last days of Rome than he is for health and fitness." Neil chugged what I assumed was his fourth expresso of the day. His hands shook.

"What does that even mean? The Head of Leisure. It's hardly a proper job." Neil stopped his almost frantic search for who knows what. "Can you remember all the places he said he worked before?"

"Worked is the wrong verb. I remember our song." I hoped Neil would crack a smile at the thought of our Proclaimer's Mash up. Creating that song had been the most fun I'd had in a long time, and that was five months ago.

That can't be right. Ron and I must have had fun in all that time.

Come on, Jen. Think about something else….

So, I thought about what Carol said. How my brain was like my superpower. I'm sort of paraphrasing but she said it takes everything in and only later filters out what's important.

"What is it you're looking for? Maybe I can help." Me and my super brain.

The one consistent thing about Neil's work seemed to be the sifting of papers. Attempts were made to dry them out, rather just throw them in confidential waste. My super brain realised that he must be looking for something. Even though most things were electronic now, aren't they?

"I don't know." Neil scanned the debris. "But Chris comes here most days looking for it."

"Chris is looking for something?" It struck me that it wasn't in Neil's nature to be helpful. So why was he so eager to find it first?

"It's obviously just a distraction. Chris can hide out here and claim the big bucks. Is he still doing Tuesday and Thursdays at Woodbank?" My super brain had only just noticed that when Chris showed me out of the office there the other day he had turned the wrong way for the exit. He'd laughed it off with 'these places all look the same' - but they didn't. Not at all.

Neil looked at me with a hatred that would have burned a thousand suns. "Look Jen, it's not that I don't enjoy the persistent interruptions but I really have to get on."

"And do what?" This was the modern day equivalent to re-arranging the deck chairs on the Titanic - when the ship had already sunk to the bottom of the ocean.

Neil sat on a pile of boxes. "I can't remember if I've checked these."

"For what?"

He shrugged again. Not really talking to me.

"He's probably just looking for all the ruined chocolate as he leaf's though all his healthy eating propaganda, right?" Neil tried to dismiss it but there was an edge to his tone. As though he didn't know what Chris was looking for but, he suspected.

CHAPTER 14

"Who are you here to see?" Brian pulled the spectacles to the end of his nose and began the power play. On each and every occasion he pretended not to remember me, I was so forgettable. So unimportant.

Brian stood confidently in his handmade Italian suit. He claimed the shoes were made by the former actor Daniel Day Lewis. I considered Brian more of a bouncer than a businessman.

"Ron," I repeated. He had expected a subdued 'Mr. Smith'.

Bulldog Brian had been Ron's deputy and personal bodyguard for three months, and he hated me. Partly because of my toxic personality but, mostly, because I think he fancies Ron. When Brian first arrived it was the proper little bromance. Ron was all 'Brian this...' and 'Brian that...'. 'Brian has worked across several local authorities and managed extensive budgets'. 'Brian has headed up ethics committees and financial regulators'. 'Brian never shredded six months of financial reports' or 'spilt his coffee and shut down the server'. Good old

Brian. Ok, I think I'd actually said, 'Brian's an asshole', but it's much the same thing.

I wasn't sure what Brian did within the organisation but, from all Ron's boasting, it felt like he was pretty overqualified to do it. Hence my assumption; Brian worked here because he fancied Ron.

"Mr. Smith is very busy." Brian admonished me like I was a small child.

"I'm aware of that." I tried to sound confident and failed.

I wanted to tell the Bulldog Ron was never too busy for me but there wasn't time for us at home. I don't know why I would think it would be different at work.

Brian's slim fit suit showed off his toned physique. His salt and pepper hair matched the impeccably groomed beard. I should be describing Brian as conventionally handsome but there was something about his demeanour that was fundamentally off-putting. Ron claimed Brian wore bifocals. It seemed more likely he just liked looking down his nose at people. Particularly me.

I'd felt bad that I'd hated Brian the second I met him. Or, I'd grown enough as a person to realise I should feel bad about it. Carol had reminded me of Gran's little mantra, 'Better felt than telt'. I used to think it was Gran's preferred fabric for her array of natty tartan skirts. Then, I worried it meant I had to feel Brian.

Carol had rolled her eyes. 'Years ago, some psychologists got some experienced gamblers to play a rigged game of poker.'

'Why?'

Carol had shrugged. 'That's just how they get their kicks.' She took a large gulp of wine. 'They hooked the gamblers up to all this equipment to measure their bodies' responses to the game.'

It was a thrilling conversation. Even the hamster was too bored to juggle.

'Way before they said the game was rigged, even before they reported thinking it, there were changes in their physiology.'

I'd wondered if this was going to be in the test. I probably should have been taking notes.

'So, when you get an uneasy feeling around someone; listen to it. Your body often picks up on something before your brain does.'

I wasn't sure what knowledge Carol had sought to impart but I felt like I'd been green lit to be a bitch. I wondered if Carol was giving me more credit than I deserved. I'd just had one too many penis on the handbag incidents from Pervy Pete at the bus stop to be naively optimistic about strangers. Still, maybe I should listen to my super brain on this one. Unusually, all it could see in that moment was Brian.

CHAPTER 15

"Have you got your old job back?" David, my former line manager, looked ready to resign. I saw a glint of hope in his eye at the thought of my return as we sat in the break room at Smiths. I had avoided this place like the plague when I worked here. All my breaks were spent 'off-site'. I'd spent more time in this room once I left.

With Brian gone I was able to see other things. Paint peeling from the walls. Free coffee replaced by a vending machine where people had to pay. A tatty old kettle and toaster that looked as if it had been found by the bins. This was not the clinically clean Smiths I remembered.

"Have those been PAT tested?" I was concerned more than anything. My work place had just burnt to the ground I didn't want Ron's facing the same problem. Or did I? Maybe then there would be more time for us.

David moved in front of the dodgy electrical devices. "Someone brought them in from home."

I imagined the someone to be him now that he spent more nights at Janice's. Ron would have a full set of kitchen appliances to return to.

"That microwave looks like something from the opening scene of *Casualty.*"

The whole place felt like it should be condemned.

"Are there still Danish pastries on a Friday?" My voice nervous as I tried to distract the train of thoughts. I couldn't admit I wasn't sure what day it was – or that, even if it was Friday, I wouldn't want to eat anything in this place.

Dave laughed bitterly. "Jen, there aren't even Fridays anymore."

Janice handed me a coffee.

"Did you have to pay for this?"

"It's safer than the kettle." Janice nodded to the black scorch mark on the base. "I got a shock from that last week. Not that I'm complaining. It was sort of good to feel alive again."

Janice looked tired. Her always impeccably manicured nails were chipped and had a distinctive home done look.

"We haven't been out for ages. You fancy catching up for a drink after work?" It felt like we weren't safe to talk here.

Janice and David exchanged a look.

"What was that look?" I challenged.

Janice smiled, looked me directly in the eye, and tried to communicate something. Something that wasn't about me.

"There isn't a lot of after work at the moment. You know what it's like."

I thought of Ron, alone in the study, night after night. Even at weekends. Maybe especially at weekends. Our dinners with Caitlin were the only real time we spent together.

"It may be rose tinted glasses but I don't remember the place looking as rough as this. What's happened here?"

Another glance exchanged.

"Jen couldn't make it past Ron's new work wife." Janice had found me when I had wandered into the office hoping to see a friendly face after the confrontation with the Bull Dog.

"Don't call him that." Brian already had more status than I did.

"It's not what I usually call him." Janice growled.

"Does Ron have a photograph of me on his desk?" He had one of us as his screensaver on his phone. I wondered if it was just Brian who didn't know who I was.

"Clear desk policy." Janice growled again.

"Clear office policy but the looks of it?" The place felt like was empty.

"Text him." David handed me my phone that had been lying on the desk. "Ron will be furious."

I wasn't sure that Ron would feel anything about what had just happened. Or, worse, he would be angry at me for disturbing him. I often wondered why I never just breezed into the study at night. It felt like there was an invisible force field around Ron.

"Ron is busy." I tried to sound compassionate to myself too; I was not busy. Not at all.

David and Janice both acknowledged that once I left Smiths was devoid of entertainment. Well, they'd said 'disasters' but it was one and the same thing.

"I can see him later. It's not important." *It was*. It always is when people say that.

"I just thought he'd want some lunch." I'd already thrown the Happy Meal away realising it was ridiculous. It was a joke. A half-assed attempt to compete with the shower cubicle date.

"Stupid really."

"It was thoughtful." Janice defended.

Thoughtful would have been to remember Ron needed to reduce his cholesterol.

Janice looked at the burger remnants in the overflowing bin with mild repulsion. David looked as though he contemplated eating it. They looked like they could do with a decent meal and a good sleep. When we worked together Janice used to love to party but their dishevelled appearance didn't seem like the aftermath of fun.

"Ron's losing it." Janice snapped.

David caught her eye.

David, the clear office choice for any deputy manager position. This Brian had blown in from nowhere.

"Have you seen the penis extension that flash prick drives?" Janice scowled.

"I've always wanted a Lotus." David looked genuinely broken and, for a split second, I resented Ron too. What was he thinking? Brian over David?

"You wouldn't be with me driving that clown car." Janice snapped again. Defending David against his own implied criticism.

I was too long in the tooth to hang around for other people's domestics. "I think I'm going to go."

Although, again it troubled me. "If Brian can afford to drive around in a flash sports car why is he working here?"

"Because I was a serial killer in a former life." Dave sighed. "Karma is punishing me."

"Janice would be the serial killer, surely." I smiled but my face felt hollow at the gesture. All of us looked dreadful. Yet none of us said that out loud.

"Brian is much more qualified than me."

"Yeah." It still troubled me. "Don't you think too qualified?"

No one seemed to care.

"You should stay. Ron would want to see you." David didn't sound convinced. Brian, much as we all hated him, seemed to know Ron's mind better than any of us.

David looked to the floor. He knew I'd spotted the lie.

"It seems quieter today." I looked around the office that had once bustled with people. I thought how I could tactfully ask about their appearance. Janice looked particularly grim.

"It's quiet most days. A few people have left, others have reduced their hours."

"No one empty the bins either?"

"No." Dave watched a few flies buzz around the waste.

I wasn't entirely sure what Smiths did but there had been lots of people clamouring to do it. Ron had only employed me out of some kind of morbid fascination. He thought I had some Machiavellian plan to take the place down. LOL, right?

"Are you ok?" Janice looked genuinely concerned.

I wanted to cry. The encounter with Brian was humiliating.

"You look like crap."

I wondered if Janice thought I looked worse than they did.

David nudged her.

"Well, more crappy than usual." She tried to be flippant.

"I've been hearing that a lot lately." At least the sheen of the building was gone. No reflection of the truth here. "You guys don't look so good either."

Janice's eyes filled with tears. Dave turned away.

"I'm concerned." Not just being a bitch like back in the old days.

"I know." Janice sounded as though concern was worse.

Another quick check for drones in the office then David sat down. He placed his arm around Janice.

"Ron is still Ron." It sounded more like he was trying to convince himself. "It's just...."

"Yeah, yeah. There's a lot going on." Juggle hamster, juggle.

Janice looked thoughtfully at her coffee. "It's a lot of money, Jen. If you were still here I'd kind of assume it was your cock up."

She was being generous. It could be part of my legacy.

"What's a lot of money?"

"Why are you still here?" The unmistakable bark of Brian made us all jump.

CHAPTER 16

"He didn't ask you to leave." Ron seemed almost annoyed. "Brian's job is to make sure everyone remains focused."

Ron was taking his side!

"He terrified Janice and David into submission. Haven't you stopped to think why all your staff are leaving?"

"Who said they're leaving?" Ron snapped.

I could feel the tears sting the back of my eyes as I stepped back in horror. "Well, what the Hell was happening at the office today? A massive game of hide and seek. It was like a ghost ship." My voice matched his defensive tone.

"Sorry," Ron stepped forward. "I'm sorry I snapped." He tried to take my hand but I stepped further back.

"Jen, I'm sorry. It's been a really long day. Can we talk about something else?"

"Like?" It felt like Ron and I were running out of things to say. Too many topics were now taboo.

"Should we be talking about anything else? This feels really important. Have you seen the state of Janice and David? What's happening?" To them. To us.

It was half past eight in the evening and Ron had only just got home. He had eaten at the office, again. Increasingly our meals with Caitlin were the only time we ate together. Ron was often leaving for work just as I was getting up. It would be a quick coffee now before hours in the study. Some nights I wasn't entirely sure he had even come to bed.

"If you're not happy." I didn't want to say it. I didn't even want to think it but the past few years had taught me problems don't just go away by ignoring them. "If there's a problem with us then we need to talk about it and, you need to stop taking it out on everyone else."

"You can't really think there's a problem with us?"

For a moment, I wondered if Ron had been living in a different flat, with a different person. I wondered how he could look at our life and realise there wasn't an issue.

"None of this is about us." Ron protested.

It was becoming about us.

"There's just so much going on at work."

The blanket statement from the man who made me promise that I wouldn't push him away.

I didn't want to talk about Smiths. I hadn't even wanted to mention I was at the office today but it's hard to be intellectually stimulating for your partner after hours of watching Daytime TV. I was trying to keep my

102

brain occupied to stop the cray cray leaking out. I'd read a rather informative article about how avocados aren't strictly vegan. Apparently the whole avocado growing process relies on the sexual exploitation of bees. They're essentially trafficked across the country.

Ron hadn't shared my indignation. 'You don't even like avocado.'

'That's not the point.' I was still unreasonably angry with him.

'Fine.' He sensed it. 'We'll stop eating avocados'.

No-one should eat avocados. Avocados are for tools. Caitlin, needless to say, had smashed avocado and toast for breakfast. I mean, come on, what's wrong with Coco Pops?

Grown-ups don't eat kids cereal for breakfast. That was her exact comment when she found out I'd eaten all of Joey's cereal.

I was trying to be an adult. I was trying to have a boring conversation about bees. Ron seemed to find that more tedious that my unregulated self. The whole incident at Smiths left me (perhaps) even more unreasonably annoyed with Ron. Brian's dismissal of me from the office only piled on further insult and now, after a hard day for us both, we were arguing.

Ron took his glasses off and massaged his temples; probably wishing he'd stuck to the bee conversation.

Another headache. I should let it go. Encourage him to have a paracetamol and a lie down but, I'd already been told, there were more papers to read.

103

"Janice and David are our friends." I backed down, a little, and began rubbing his shoulders as I reached for the painkillers. The box was almost finished again.

"Well, maybe we should keep our get-togethers for social time." Ron sighed, hearing how it sounded. "I just meant...."

"Yeah, there's a lot going on." I pulled out his trusted mantra. "And everyone is really busy and important. Bar me."

"It's not like that." He protested, or he felt that he should. His tone was flat. A half-assed attempt to placate a petulant overgrown child with no direction, no job and no bloody clue what to do next.

Ron tried to reach out and take my hand but I stepped away. This was pity.

"I didn't pop in to see Janice and David. I came to see you but, I couldn't get past the Bulldog."

"He doesn't like it when you call him that." Ron's tone defensive again.

"Then maybe he should try some personality dialysis. David was the natural choice for your next in command. Why did you overlook him?"

I'd never questioned Ron about his business before. I'd never had that much of an interest. Not even when I worked there. If I had I'd have known about Smiths underwriting my business loan. Sometimes you have to pay attention to the small print. Not with the important stuff like online shopping and privacy contracts but with the boring financial stuff that no one really cares about.

Ron looked anxious. "It's complicated."

I wanted to accept his explanation but everyone knew that little soundbite is what people throw out when they are being less than transparent.

"You mean I wouldn't understand it." I snapped.

"No. That's not what I meant." Ron tried to soften his tone but the frustration was evident.

"I know you're finding it hard being out of work. You just need something to focus your creative edge."

As though all my problems were so easily solved.

"You're a talented woman. You should be thinking about what the next big adventure is."

"Really?" I could feel a lump form in my throat. "What am I good at, Ron?"

Silence.

"I know there's a lot going on at Smiths." I grabbed my coat. "But, in case you haven't noticed Mr. Genius, there's a lot going on here too."

CHAPTER 17

"You're going back?" Mum anxiously handed me a tissue.

I'd moved back in with my parents before. It wasn't horrendous but we were all pretty close to the edge. Do you know what parricide is? It's the killing of one's parents. I'd googled it. That's how close to the edge we were.

"It's my flat." I wiped the tears away from my eyes. Ron would appreciate the time to look over the vital papers. Or, perhaps with me gone there would be no need to banish himself to the spare room.

"Maybe." I had to push the words out. "Maybe I should ask him to stay at his place for a bit."

"Is that what you want?" Mum asked without judgement.

"No," but, I didn't want life to continue like this either.

"It's not like we'd see less of each other." Maybe if Ron and I lived separately we would have to plan time to be together. Maybe he would realise then our relationship wasn't worth the effort.

"Maybe all of this would be less important if I had a job. I feel useless."

"You're not useless!" Mum hugged me again.

I wanted to believe her but parents have to say that. Whether my adult existence was the results of my genes or environment, my life outcomes were on them. Besides, whenever I cry I think Mum sees 5-yearold Jen who wants to be a zookeeper and look after the giraffes.

I should have gone to Carol. Carol would have told me to man up then one of us would have launched into a diatribe about gender politics and why people are never told to 'woman up' or even 'human up'. See, even now, as my life is falling apart, I can't focus. Perhaps if I had taken the pills the doctor had been so keen on during my teenage years, I would have been able to focus on the world falling apart around me rather than just stare, confused, at the remnants. If I could have focussed maybe I wouldn't have had to just watch it all happen either. Maybe I could have stopped it.

It was the 'creative edge' comment that pushed me over. My parents affectionately call it the 'cray cray' (because that's nicer than crazy). It all means the same thing.

"I wish I was normal."

Mum laughed. "There's no such thing as 'normal', love. And, if there is, it means only one thing - not special."

My specialness was exhausting.

"He's tired of my unique outlook on the world."

107

I was the novelty that soon wore off.

"It sounds like he was really busy." Mum sounded unsure. Ron's behaviour and attitude was indefensible. Or was it me, getting it all wrong, again?

"I didn't notice Stephen and I drifting apart." I told myself work was the problem. What if it wasn't? Maybe throwing himself into work was Ron's solution to the real problem; us. Maybe it wasn't about the papers.

"That was different." Mum protested, without any real certainty.

Everyone wants to think their current relationship is different from the last because that had ended. The harsh truth was that this relationship might end too.

"Your Dad heard rumours that things weren't going well at Smiths."

I couldn't imagine where Dad would have heard that.

"Maybe you should try and talk to him about it."

I had tried. Although, thinking about it now, I couldn't remember the last time Ron and I had talked. We used to spend hours talking about everything and nothing. If things weren't going well at Smiths then Ron should have told me.

"When was the last time you saw Ron?"

Mum shrugged. "He's busy, love."

Not too busy for a weekly dinner with Caitlin.

He was stepping back from me, my life and all that was supposed to have become our life.

Ron was too busy to see the people who were important to me but it was inconceivable we would miss a dinner with Caitlin.

"This isn't the life that I want." I didn't want to have to convince any partner that I was important too.

"What did Dad hear about Smiths? Where did he hear it?"

A look flashed across her face. "I don't know, love. I don't really understand financial things."

"And, Dad does?" Whatever he had heard he would have got it wrong.

"He just heard that things weren't going well."

At work or at home.

"Remember love, the ship doesn't sink because it's surrounded by water. The ship sinks when the water gets inside." She pulled out Carols' trusted mantra that Mum had attributed to getting me out of my bed during my last emotional crisis and making me face the world again. She forgets Carol physically dragged me from the bed.

"You need to steady yourself in this storm."

"So you think there is an oncoming storm?"

"I'm worried things are getting on top of you. A little bit."

Mum was right. She always was. Last week I had googled 'self-care'. Good Lord Google suggested a relaxing walk in the woods. That's when I'd thought it would be more relaxing if I took Caitlin, an axe and a shovel.

"Maybe there is one good thing." I wiped the tears away with my sleeve. "Caitlin's no longer our biggest problem."

CHAPTER 18

It was late when I finally returned home. I'd left my parents about half ten but had gone to one of those trendy all night coffee places that are probably just a front for human trafficking and drug dealing. The guy behind the counter looked angry and bitter with life. So the place really suited my mood.

Mum was anxious to know I was home so I text her I was. I said Ron was asleep and I was going to bed. I told Ron I was still at my parents. I told myself I just needed more time but, I couldn't face going home so, I lied to the people I loved.

"Jen." Chris noticed me sitting alone at the door of the café.

"Jen." He repeated. Louder this time as he looked anxiously at the door. I could have sworn he made a gesture with his hand. As though to shoo someone else away.

"What are you doing here?" He appeared friendly. Maybe even concerned.

"Who was that?" I looked outside to try and catch sight of the figure that had fled from the door.

Chris stared at the space vacantly. There was a wild look in his eyes.

"Jen, it's the middle of the night. What are you doing out?"

"It's 2018, Chris. Women can do what they like." I snapped.

I had lied to Mum. I had lied to Ron. What would a lie to Chris matter?

"I couldn't sleep."

He looked at the almost vat of coffee sitting on the table in front of me. "That'll help."

Oddly, it usually does.

"No coffee in your swanky new flat?"

It wasn't that swanky.

"None that tastes like cat's piss. Reminds me of work." I quipped.

Leaving the house in the middle of the night for awful coffee as a cure for insomnia was just bizarre. I might have to ask this man for a reference. That stopped me from just telling him to get lost.

"What are you doing on the dawn patrol?" I tried to shift focus from my implausible tale of events. I wondered whether I should text Neil. Or, if Chris would tell him about this odd encounter.

I didn't really care why Chris was out in the middle of the night. He was clearly with someone he didn't want me to see. A shadowy figure who had not only backed away from the doorway but had actually run away down the street. Either I was about to find out Chris was into some kinky stuff with sex workers or, worse, I was about to see him as an actual human being.

"Working late." Chris brazened on. "Why I get paid the big bucks."

Maybe he wasn't an asshole. Maybe Chris just had years of hurt that meant he came across like an asshole so people didn't want to get close. Only, there was no humility to how he said it. No forced bravado.

I should have asked what had kept Chris at work until this time. He seemed to find it challenging to fill a working day never mind extend it.

"Who was that?" I repeated the question and stared out into the darkness.

Chris looked around pretending too hard to be puzzled. "No-one."

A better lie would have been to say he hadn't seen anyone. He dismissed the significance of the person rather than their existence.

As Chris stepped closer I detected the pungent smell of alcohol on his breath. "I think I'll give the coffee a miss." He looked at my cup. "Thanks for the honest evaluation."

The dingy surroundings and sign hanging from the front of the building had been the honest appraisal of the service and menu.

I had been crying. It was obvious that I had been crying and, yet, he said nothing. Maybe he was trying to respect my privacy. Or, maybe, given how awful I'd looked for weeks, this little sight was expected.

113

"Do you want to join me?"

Please say no, please say no.

Chris paused for a moment. He looked as though he was genuinely considering it. He shook his head and moved towards the door.

"You know, Jen, none of this was ever personal." He caught my eye in an evasive way. To anyone else it might have sounded like an apology. Or, recognition that our working relationship had not been the best. If I'm honest I know people with a far higher BMI than Chris but he gained his unkind nickname because Neil and I didn't like him. For a heartbeat I recognised that perhaps we were the bad guys.

I opened my mouth to say something. Apologise maybe. Recognise that just because he was a dickhead, I didn't have to be.

Chris sneered as he left triumphant. "Give old Ron my best, would you?"

"Asshole." I called out, a bit too loud.

The man behind the counter looked up and nodded. "He's been coming in here most nights for the past few weeks. Usually with another guy."

I didn't want to ask. "He doesn't have blond tips in his hair?"

The guy behind the counter laughed. "Nah."

At least I knew it wasn't Neil.

CHAPTER 19

I wandered slowly back to the flat questioning whether the road home had always felt so dark and lonely.

I wanted to message Neil and tell him about the encounter with Chris but, it was well past midnight and it felt like we didn't have that kind of relationship anymore. Besides, there was too much to explain. Too much that I didn't understand. Neil would focus on all the wrong parts of the story. Like why I was out in the middle of the night drinking coffee, alone? Or, he wouldn't care and that would hurt more.

Ron had tried to call again. I texted to say I was still at my parents. I asked him not to call as it would upset them. I felt compelled to reply to the incessant calls. He'd worry. Or, he'd call my parents and they'd worry. What did it matter where I was? Ron didn't care that we sat night by night in different rooms.

I wondered if Ron was the type of guy who would never leave. The kind that you had to make go. I felt sick at the thought as I walked the final few paces to the front door. My stomach clenched as I pushed the door handle down. The world began to spin around me.

Ron had waited up. Sitting on the sofa, as Mum had predicted, 'NetFlixing and chilling by himself.' I really needed to explain that term to her.

Papers were strewn across the coffee table but, I had the sense he'd been unable to focus. I tried to pay more attention to what was on them but it was a jumble of numbers and red pen, highlights and arrows scrawled everywhere. Maybe Ron was losing the plot. Put this lot on a pinboard, connect it with red string and it would look like the work of a serial killer. Although I think we're supposed to say serial murderer now, aren't we?

"I'm sorry." Ron leapt up. "Jen, I am so sorry." He held out his arms and I tried to resist but, suddenly, I was in them, crying.

"It was so amazing that you dropped in to see me. Brian was a dickhead. I don't know why I defended him but, we're in a bit of a hole at Smith's and he seems to know how to get us out of it."

"Please, don't cry." Ron held me closer as he wiped away the wears. "The last thing I would ever want to do is hurt you."

I could see Brian charging people a pound for coffee and driving around in his flash prick car.

"I shouldn't have bothered you. You're busy and I'm completely surplus." We were falling over each other to accept responsibility for this latest feud.

Ron looked into my eyes. "You are not surplus, Jen. You are the centre of my world. I know I am working hellish hours and I am constantly distracted but I'm doing this for us."

"Don't let Brian hear that." I let a smile brush my lips. "I'm sorry I'm around all the time."

Ron needed space. That was something that was impossible to find in the tiny flat. Only, we'd never needed that space before.

"I want you around all the time!" Ron wiped the tears from my face. "I don't want to work like this. Live our lives like this. I was hoping to pull back but, it can't be right now. Work is horrendous."

I'd never heard Ron describe anything as horrendous. A word I used all the time - two days ago to describe a new breakfast cereal. Ron, on the other hand, described the occasion when his knee had swollen up to three times its usual size and had to have a hole drilled in it to drain the fluid out as 'quite unpleasant'. We were very different people.

Maybe too different.

"Maybe you could come in sometime and help out…." Ron ventured.

"Would that be helpful?" I still wasn't entirely sure what the problem was and couldn't be confident I hadn't caused it. It felt like Ron was increasingly unwilling to explain it all to me.

"What is going on?"

He looked so tired.

"I could come and help. If you wanted."

Neither of us wanted that. Neither of us were convinced that more time together was the solution.

"I just want to protect you from all the crap that's going on so, when I come back here, to our little world, I can forget it."

That's not working. They're not two different worlds. It's the same one.

At Smiths the word 'liability' had followed me around. By the time I left I was barely trusted to make the tea. I didn't want to go back there. Especially with that kettle.

Ron was working more hours than felt humane. He said he wanted to pull back, but what did I want? My partner getting ready to retire when I don't feel like I've even started.

You're in different places. Chris words echoed through the air between us.

"It's not because you weren't the model, whatever it was you were supposed to be doing," Ron smiled. He knew we both needed a way out of this.

"Smiths problems shouldn't stop you pursuing your dreams."

I didn't have any dreams; not anymore.

"I don't feel quite finished at the Centre." I broke in with another excuse. "There's something niggling at me."

Ron's eyes glazed over. He knew it was time to move on. The whole world knew it.

"And, I don't know. Maybe Neil could find me something else."

Ron looked more hopeful. Strange, given that he'd cautiously suggested on a few occasions I didn't need to work. He'd been shot down in flames but always left it open for me to try something completely different. Ron just saw how cray cray unemployed Jen could be. He was eager to have her gainfully employed and, more importantly, out of the way.

I wasn't sure if I was offering us a way out or digging us in deeper. We'd apologised. We'd made up. But this time, a bit of the distance remained.

CHAPTER 20

"What do you mean, the CCTV is missing?" This morning had been crappy enough.

Ron had been on his phone and laptop since I woke up at 5am. The atmosphere was still strained. We were both on our best behaviour. Reinforcing the gulf between us. We'd never had to put on a show before. So the last thing I needed was Fireman Sam and his sidekick rocking up and derailing my careers intervention from Neil at what was left of the Community Centre. This pair hadn't made a positive impression the night of the fire. One of them had sucked air in through his teeth. 'Aye, it's a big yin,' he'd offered as the world blazed around us. All that training clearly hadn't gone to waste.

The Fire Inspector sat Neil and I down. We were just about to head for coffee. So their presence was even more inconvenient.

"I'm not sure how else I can explain it." He looked at the little work experience guy (at least, he looked about 12. Was I getting old?).

"The CCTV footage of the night of the fire is gone." He spoke slower.

"You mean it's been destroyed?" Neil went to check for the disc.

"I mean it is not there. Unless it was never there." The Inspector looked as bored as I was by this discussion.

I had to let this go. I had to trust the authorities and move on. Only, if this was the authorities I didn't trust them to prove that fire is hot.

"I heard you didn't do the Fire safety training." The Inspector looked at me accusingly.

"Was CCTV training part of that?" I wasn't being the fall guy for this. "No-one touches the CCTV. If the disc isn't there…" Well, I really didn't know what that meant.

"I thought you didn't work here anymore." The work experience guy looked at me accusingly.

"She's with me." Neil growled. "Any ideas what could have happened to the disc?" He directed the question to me.

I shrugged. I hadn't really thought about the security details of the Centre.

"Chris always checks the CCTV." Neil appeared to be talking to himself.

"Does he?" I wasn't really aware of Chris being responsible for anything.

"He was always fiddling with it." Neil looked angrily at the melted monitors. "Don't you remember?"

We couldn't get moving for Chris. He was all over everything else. Why not the CCTV?

I laughed. "Oh, yeah. The time we caught him checking out the changing rooms."

Chris had claimed he was setting up the cameras. He set them up in some pretty odd areas if you ask me but, apparently, no one did.

"It wasn't anything sinister." Neil pulled his hand through his hair. The blonde tips made his hair matt together. His fingers stuck. "It was just a joke we had." Neil pulled his hand to free it from his hair. Wads of blonde strands came with it.

"Chris wanted to move the office." I remember it was the one and only time I saw him care about anything. "He wanted to use a newer part of the building and use this place for storage."

It didn't make sense. People would have to move all the equipment through busy hallways. At least, they would have been busy if anyone ever used the Centre.

"The whole office would have been destroyed then." Somehow, that felt significant.

Neil glared at me, as though I had inadvertently said too much.

"It's pretty destroyed now." The work experienced quipped.

The office was still standing; unlike other parts of the building.

"You guys probably shouldn't hang around here so much. All the debris."

Maybe that was why I felt so crap all the time.

"Chris." The Inspector took out his notebook. "The fat guy?"

Neil nodded.

"He's not that fat." I whispered a protest; still disturbed about our encounter last night. There was had been something sinister in Chris's voice when he spoke about Ron.

"He didn't spend as much time at the other Centres." The Inspector checked his notes.

"Tuesdays and Thursdays he was at Woodbank. Just down the road." Neil began to pace. We looked forward to the days we knew Chris would not be in attendance. It was like a kind of respite.

The Inspector checked his notes. "No, he didn't."

Neil looked him, as though his life depended on it. "He told us every Tuesday and Thursday."

"That's not what he told me." The Inspector, more to calm Neil down, checked his notes again.

"Why would he lie?" Neil was increasingly angry.

It was evident why Chris had lied. Slacking off. I just couldn't work out why Neil was so emotionally invested in it.

"What did he say he was doing?" Neil tried to get a look at the Inspectors notebook.

"Confidentiality." He flipped the book closed.

The legislation people call on when there's something to hide.

The Inspector gritted his teeth. "I just need to sort out the CCTV mess. I don't need to work out what your boss was or was not doing when he should have been at work."

"Where did he tell you he was?" I wasn't as interested in Chris whereabouts as I was to Neil's reaction to the news. "And where do you think he was?" I directed the second question to Neil.

Both men were silent.

"Isn't it just as important to an investigation when someone lies?" More so? Like, what are they concealing.

"He didn't necessarily lie to me." The Inspector defended.

"How do you know that?" I tried to sound casual as I stirred up the doubt in his head.

Neil held my gaze for a heartbeat. "Maybe someone moved the CCTV."

Suspiciously, Neil 'looked' with the air of a person not expecting to find it.

Was Chris looking for the CCTV footage when he appeared at the remnants of the Centre? Were the papers merely a distraction? Did Neil know before the Fire Officer told him that the CCTV was gone? With all these questions I felt like I was in a popular 90s TV drama. Any second now I should look all wistful and do a piece straight to camera. Only this wasn't a TV show. This was supposed to be my life.

Don't get involved.

"Strange place for a Leisure Centre." The Inspector looked out of the window.

"I think the theory was build it and they will come. Tends not to be the most effective business model these days."

I tried to sound all esoteric like that voice in the corn that spoke to Kevin Costner and told him to set sail on that ship…. Hang on. I may be getting two films confused.

"What was *Waterworld* about?"

The work experience guy looked confused.

"CCTV can help establish what happened." The Inspector looked set to indulge in another lengthy modelling of how to handle incompetents for his side kick.

I didn't want to be rude but if we weren't at the bakers for 11am they sell out of Yum Yums and no one wants a fruit slice in their life.

"This place is covered with cameras." *Jen, that's getting involved.* "And aren't the videos all uploaded somewhere centrally in this day and age? Some kind of cloud?"

The work experience guy looked at the CCTV monitors. "This is a very rudimentary system. Odd, given how much the council is reported to have invested in this place?"

"Reported."

"It's an old system too. For the age of the renovations." The work experience was in his element talking to the dinosaurs about technology.

The Fire Inspector shot him a look. "We're certain it is arson. And that guy Hippie Cr... Mackenzie. He was seen hanging around."

This isn't my problem. I have to move on. I have other problems.

I stood up and checked the CCTV machine too. Pointless. We already knew it was gone The Inspector said, Neil had checked. It just felt somehow incriminating if I was the only one not to look.

"Mac would have no idea about CCTV." I protested.

"He was a mechanical engineer." The 12-year-old checked his notes.

"No he wasn't!" I laughed. No one joined in.

Neil shrugged. "I think that's right."

Wow! I hadn't really thought of Mac as being anything other than homeless.

"You think he's capable of arson? He's not capable of lighting a match."

The Inspector shrugged. "He smokes."

"He wouldn't." I spoke to Mac loads when I went to my car. Ok, the first week or so he had scared the hell out of me but we sort of got on now. I'd give him tea and a shower. I don't mean I bathed him. I'm not Mother Theresa. I just let him use the facilities. Neil was forever trying to get him to go to the hostel.

The Inspector shrugged again. In his mind the matter had been concluded. "You two are off the hook."

"When were we on the hook?" Neil looked anxious.

"What evidence do you have?" If the CCTV was gone how could anyone know who'd done what. "And how would Mac have got into the office?"

Neil patted my hand. Another little helpful piece of advice from his therapist. Show more empathy. That equated to hand patting.

"Likely he removed the CCTV and burnt the building down after that." The Inspector shrugged again.

"There are traces of accelerant everywhere." The work experience chimed back in.

"Traces?" I folded my arms. "Did you see how quickly this place burned?" It was like the walls were made of fire.

"What did you mean earlier about the reported expenditure on the building? It shouldn't have burned as quickly as it did. Should it?"

"Jen." Neil's voice sounded soothing.

Neil had an inherent trust in authority. The man in the uniform said it was Mac – hence, it was Mac. If they'd tried to pin it on us Neil would probably have believed that too.

"And what?" I spoke accusingly to Neil. "Mac broke in here and took the CCTV footage, did he? Why? What did Mac have to gain with this place burning? Mac liked it here. He likes us."

The Inspector shrugged again. Not used to being questioned. "Junkies can be wiry".

CHAPTER 21

"Well, if the Fire Inspector thinks he did it." Ron continued to be distant and distracted over dinner. I'd suggested we eat out in an attempt to bridge the gulf between us. It wasn't working. I'd got dressed up, worn my best underwear. I'd even done my hair and my nails. Ron barely noticed. He barely looked up from his phone.

" 'Junkies can be wiry.' Those were his actual words."

Ron continued to check his emails.

"You've met Mac!" I wanted to knock the bloody phone from his hand. He'd never have done this months ago. Only, now it was clear that Mac was unimportant to Ron. Probably on the list of reasons he didn't want me working at the Centre.

Ron's Blackberry buzzed into action. "Sorry." He stood up. "I have to take this." He left the table. He should have done half an hour ago. He hadn't really been here all night.

I tried to engross myself in the menu but, that was pretty pointless as we'd already eaten. I'd barely touched my main course and hadn't even considered a dessert. I couldn't face a coffee. I was tired, miserable and just wanted to go home. I thought Ron would have made an effort after last night. Surely whatever was going on at Smiths could wait a few hours. It had had his attention most of today.

"Jen?" The waiter approached the table.

I smiled, trying to work out how I knew this balding, middle aged man.

"Stephen?" More of a question than recognition.

The ex who'd run off with all my money. Ah, fond memories whilst I was making even more happy ones.

This may have been the most surreal moment of my life. Stephen was our waiter. Incomprehensible. Waiting tables is hard work and Stephen's not a fan of that.

My smile vanished. Not only because of what he'd done to me all those months before but, what he'd done now to himself. Thicker round the waist, his belly hung prominently over his belt and struggled to be contained by the cheap black shirt stained with sweat under the arms. He had a wiry, unkept beard, which felt like the biggest betrayal of all. Stephen hated the game I had invented at the bookshop; 'Hipster or Homeless'. If I'd only just met Stephen it's hard to say what side of the fence I'd have come down on.

I took a sharp intake of breath. The memory of us laughing together was like a kick to the stomach. It was a simpler time. A time when life was less complicated. Or, when I was.

"Are you dining alone?" He sounded almost hopeful.

"My partner's outside."

Partner, he hadn't felt like that in weeks. Ron was fighting some kind of battle alone.

"An important business call." We both heard, 'Spending time with me isn't that important.'

It's hard to know what to say to the man who almost ruined your life. I'd done the nice goodbye. I'd left him when I was on a high. I mean, I was still at rock bottom but I was more optimistic about it.

"Could we just pay, actually?" Tonight had already been a disaster. Suggesting we go out for dinner was an attempt for more than us to be in the same place at the same time. I had thought by leaving the house all the drama of Smith's could be left behind too. The drama had followed us here.

I would be pleased to see the back of that bloody phone. Ron was supposed to be switching to an iPhone as the day dawned to a close for Blackberry. There wasn't even time for that. 'My life is on that phone', he had protested to David. I hadn't realised how true that was.

"Can't I interest you in another drink?" Stephen nodded towards the cocktail menu with a knowing smile.

"No thanks." Alcohol and cocktails was just another thing that failed to excite me now. It felt like there was so little joy left in the world. I tried to think of something that would make me feel better.

"No dessert either." Stephen shook his head. "Changed days." He smiled again, as though he still knew me. As though we were still somehow friends.

"I have a break in a few minutes." He ventured. "If you wanted to catch up."

I must have looked as horrified as I felt.

"Yeah, sorry." He shifted awkwardly. "Probably not."

I had to leave. The only thing worse than having my life fall apart was having Stephen there to witness it. Perhaps more than needing to be happy was needing Stephen to think that I was.

I reached into Ron's coat pocket to find his wallet and found instead a small hard box. Intrigued I pulled it out. Tiffany's. I took a deep breath and popped it open.

Holy shit.

CHAPTER 22

"What's that?" Stephen looked over my shoulder.

"Nothing." I threw the box back into Ron's pocket. "Just can't find his wallet. I'll get this." I handed Stephen my credit card.

"How are you?" Stephen made a performance of sorting the machine. Stalling. I didn't have time for niceties.

Ron is going to propose. That's why he's been so distracted. Bless, he's nervous. That's why he'd cleared his internet history and been so secretive. Ron would have a grand romantic gesture up his sleeve. Hence all the phone calls. Here I was blabbering on about the plight of some poor soul, down on his luck who might just be the next tragic victim of the British Justice System. Hang on, that should still matter. Shouldn't it?

The heavy sinking feeling lifted, a little. I was glad I'd made the effort tonight. Tonight wasn't about Smiths. Tonight was about us.

Oh crap, Stephen was still waiting on an answer.

"Not too bad. You?" I only asked because I felt I should. Some kind of verbal tic.

I rarely thought about Stephen now. Odd, when he had once been my entire world. The only time I considered him was in relation to the crappy thing that he did. Stephen was my past. Ron was my future. I could breathe easy. Or, at least, I should. The distance of the past few weeks had been explained. Ron was terrible at keeping secrets.

Stephen shrugged. "I still feel bad about…."

I waved my hand dismissively, but I should have let him finish. How would Stephen have explained what he did? How would I? Maybe I was only ok with the events of the past few years because I thought it had brought me to Ron. How would I feel when it all fell apart?

Jen, stop it. You're spiralling. Ron has a ring. It's not falling apart – it's falling together.

Bloody hell, that was another one of those insipid inspirational quotes from Neil's calendar. They just bleed into your brain.

Now I'd thought of Neil and was annoyed again. Focus.

Ron has a ring.

A ring won't fix this.

If he was planning to propose, why not just do it? Why spend the evening on his phone? Unless he was co-ordinating a brass band or some sky writing.

"There's not a band out there? A low flying jet?"

Stephen looked entertained. "I've missed you."

133

Relief and joy in his face. Two years too late. When we were together, towards the end, Stephen found it hard to even tolerate me.

"Was that some kind of joke?" He looked confused. "To make things less awkward?"

"Why would they be awkward?" I smiled, genuinely this time, and Stephen visibly relaxed. At least his shoulders hunched forward more – I assumed that was him relaxing now.

"It was a long time ago." That's what you are supposed to say, isn't it? When someone craps on you from a great height.

"Mum said you had a great new job." Stephen knelt down at the table. Pretend intimacy, or real, it was hard to tell.

"Yeah." I smiled. "There's been a bit of a glitch with that."

He didn't need to know. Why was I still talking? Why was I spending time with the past when the future was waiting outside. My next big adventure. Maybe that's what Ron had been hinting at. Marriage. A sentence all on its own.

Was I ready for marriage? Were Ron and I? Was anyone ever really ready? Is it just something you have to bite the bullet and do? Given the age difference, Ron and I didn't really have the time not to be ready. I could feel my chest tighten.

"I heard someone burnt the place down." Of course he knew.

Stephen fumbled again with the card machine. It really couldn't be that complicated. He'd love it if this card was declined.

"So it seems." I tried to sound light-hearted, as though none of it really mattered.

Five things. Name five things you can see, hear and smell. Grounding it's called. It's a way of managing anxiety. Not that I'm anxious. Ron was about to propose. I was supposed to be excited.

I tried to focus. All I could see was Stephen. All I could hear were his words droning on. I could smell his scent, so familiar and yet, no longer home.

"They've arrested someone...." I began.

But they're wrong.

Maybe I just had to accept the Community Centre was also part of the past. It had to be, didn't it? It literally doesn't exist anymore. Yet, even Stephen seemed a more likely candidate than Mac for arson.

"Where were you on the night of...." I stopped.

He'd been questioned by the Police. He'd gone to court. I hoped Stephen's betrayal would be the biggest of my life. It wasn't appropriate to make light of it.

"I thought you'd be married with kids by now."

Stephen always knew the buttons to press. I had almost forgotten how much anxiety he caused with his mere presence. The subtle undermining of confidence; the saying of my anxieties out loud.

"I wouldn't really have had the time." Stephen had a fairly rudimentary understanding of biology.

I hadn't thought about marriage or kids recently. I had been too happy in the present to think about the future. *When did that change with Ron?*

With Stephen I reasoned raising one child (him) was enough. Now, I'm not even sure I have the mothering instinct. If the pick and mix baby situation (collecting Brandon instead of Joey) wasn't enough evidence, one of Caitlin's friend's is pregnant. People keep rubbing her stomach and saying, 'aw'. It freaks me out. Sometimes you see limbs popping out and I can't get that scene from *Alien* out of my head.

Stephen was still waiting for a response. He wanted me to ask about the wedding ring. I realised now why he'd been waiving his hand so flamboyantly. Stephen wanted me to know he'd turned his life around because marriage equates to success in his little world. Even if it wasn't a happy one.

I wasn't going to ask.

Ron has a ring.

"Do you remember Diane?" Stephen held up his left hand.

"Does she work here?" I pretended to follow the direction of his gesture.

I remembered Diane. She was his Brian.

Stephen laughed. "She's not working. She's seven months pregnant with twins."

That's more of a litter.... Hang on, seven months?

"We used to work together."

When he worked. Before he went part-time to write his book on the zombie apocalypse. I thought of the cover he had spent days drawing and almost laughed.

"We're married." He blushed. "Things had been simmering when we were together."

And after. When his poor, sickly mother had kept calling mine to tell her how broken Stephen was. As though we would have any say in the outcome of the trial.

"Great, do you need my pin?" What's the etiquette here? Tip or no tip? Adding adultery to his list of crimes, probably no tip. But, he does have twins on the way.

Bloody Hell, Jen. No tip!

"You used to think there was something going on, didn't you?" Stephen smiled. "Maybe you knew before we did."

Unlikely, that would have implied I cared.

When did I stop caring? Stephen had regained his cocky demeanour. No longer pretending to be the broken shell that had tried to make amends; tried to get me back.

"That's nice." Neil gave me that little verbal tic. When you don't know what to say, say that. Unless, you know, someone tells you they've lost a loved one. Then you use the other little gem, 'I'm sorry to hear that'. Still not sure I'd chosen the right sentiment.

"I heard you're dating some old guy?" Stephen laughed casually. As though he hadn't planned this meeting a hundred times in his head. "Must be painful seeing me at my buffest." Stephen pretended to flex his muscles. He was being playful. Too much water had passed under the bridge for that.

It was painful to see him. A ghost from the past. A potent reminder that you can love someone and then, just not. I hadn't noticed falling out of love with Stephen. I hadn't really noticed his blossoming relationship with Diane. I suddenly wondered again why Ron kept closing his lap-top and hiding his phone whenever I passed. Sometimes when couples get engaged then married, it's because they know the relationship is already over. Or one of them is pregnant.

"How long have you been married?" I smiled, triumphantly but deep down, it just felt petty.

Stephen's face fell.

I wanted to apologise, take it back but it could never be unsaid. I was supposed to be above this.

"This is a nice place." I looked around the restaurant. It was fine but, given the disastrous evening with Ron I hated it well before Stephen rocked up.

"Yeah." He glanced around, briefly. Stephen always had higher ambitions. "It's only until I get the writing off the ground."

I noticed how tired he looked. For Stephen too the day didn't have enough hours. It was exhausting being so unhappy. I tried again not to look at my own reflection in the mirrored table surface.

"Life's what happens when your making other plans. Isn't that what people say?" Another cliché from Neil's calendar.

Stephen smiled, appreciatively. "Something like that." For a moment his eyes seemed to glisten with tears. "Oh Jen, how the Hell did we come to this?"

"I need to ask you something…" Ron's voice broke in urgently. I hadn't even noticed him return.

Stephen and I jumped.

"Him!" Stephen looked horrified and, suddenly, he was the victim again.

"Not here." I stood up. "Not now."

This wasn't the story I wanted to tell people. My question to Stephen still hung in the air and left a bitter taste in my mouth. Yet, surely if this was how life should be then it shouldn't matter when Ron asked me to marry him or how.

Ron looked confused. "I need to ask you," he ploughed on. "Do you mind if we go home?"

139

CHAPTER 23

"New York?"

"I had mentioned this could be a possibility." Ron continued to calmly pack his case.

I would have remembered if New York had been mentioned as a 'possibility'.

"I urgently need to ...." He paused. "Are you interested in this?"

Not particularly. "How long will you be gone?"

There was only one case. He hadn't asked me to go. I had no job, nowhere else to be and he still hadn't asked.

"It should only be a couple of weeks." He didn't sound certain.

"Weeks?"

Silence.

"Do you know who that waiter was?" My voice cracked.

Ron continued to pack.

"It was Stephen."

He stopped and looked up. Finally, I had his attention. "Oh, I thought I recognised him. That must have been weird."

"Yeah." Made weirder by this.

"Still, we were eating at the table and he was serving so, does that mean we win? I'm joking Jen!" Ron smiled. "Clearly the book still hasn't made its millions."

"It's been so long since you made a joke. It was hard to tell."

Ron had been spending too much time with Caitlin. Ron never used to think he was better than anyone else. It was one of the many things I respected about him.

"I felt sorry for him." I shouldn't have admitted that out loud. Stephen was my ex. I shouldn't admit to any feelings for him.

Ron paused, but only briefly.

Stephen looked terrible. Of course, I shouldn't care but, maybe, a tiny part of me still did. Ron didn't have to be jealous of Stephen. Our relationship had ended. Ron's marriage to Laura had been tragically cut short. Maybe that was the real reason the ring stayed in his pocket. Marrying me would be like a betrayal.

Ron placed his arms around me uninterested in Stephen. "I know it is crappy, terrible timing but I have to go."

Ron looked at me intently. As though he was going to say something life changing. Something that neither of us wanted to hear.

"I'm going to miss Caitlin's birthday. I'll need to nip around tomorrow morning with her present." He drifted away again.

"I'm sorry to hear that." I don't think my response appropriately conveyed how ecstatic I was he should be considering her feelings.

"Is there anything else you wanted to say to me tonight?"

The ring was still in his pocket. What could be more important than that?

Ron looked confused, "like what?"

I shrugged.

Ron pulled me down beside him on the bed. "I don't want to go Jen, but it's chaos. And it's big. Really big." He looked older. Dark circles around slightly sunken eyes.

I didn't want him to go. I wasn't sure he was going to be ok. Or, that we were.

"What's going on, Ron?"

He sighed, resting his head against mine. "It's complicated."

"And you think I'm too stupid to understand it?"

"No." He protested. "I just don't think I'm smart enough to explain it."

He looked broken. A little bit more so that Stephen did. I had found pity for my ex and ignored the torment of Ron.

"Can I help?" Doubtful but, I had to ask

He rested his head against mine. "You already do."

Six months and we'd never spent a night apart. Now, when things feel at their most fragile, he was going to New York.

CHAPTER 24

Chris was bulldozing around the office looking all officious. He hated the fact that I'd been here when the Fire Crew announced their findings. He'd spent five minutes banging on about 'due process'. I thought the vein at the side of his temple was actually going to rupture. He'd taken several deep breaths, 're-evaluated his priorities' and decided a nice little neat report was required. His role now was to 'mediate' the findings and to ensure the actual report never saw the light of day.

"Aren't you at all worried that someone was in here and took the CCTV?" This wasn't my business. Why was I even here?

Because you don't want to be home without him.

Chris smiled, copying the human emotion of calm. "This isn't really your problem now, Jen. Why don't you join Ron on the golf course? The Council one, of course."

"Bit late to be advertising our services." I snipped, angry again at his mention of Ron. There was that unpleasant edge I detected before. I just couldn't place what it was.

"That's not what I meant." He sneered.

Ron wasn't on the golf course. Not content with flying to New York later this evening he had more urgent meetings in the office. No time for us anymore.

Time for Caitlin of course. He was going to see her with the birthday present. I should have been relieved that I didn't have to go and, I was; but it was a temporary reprieve. Her birthday meal was tonight.

Neil the bloody gossip must have told Chris about Ron and I. Despite what he claims.

"What did the Fire Inspector mean about the reported cost of the building?" I tried to distract myself with the mundane.

"Why do you care?" Chris challenged; more openly hostile than before. Perhaps he too knew my relationship with Ron was failing; there was no need to tolerate me now.

"Let Neil deal with all of this." Chris tried to level his tone.

"Where is Neil?" I barked; annoyed about his double betrayal. Telling and then, lying about telling.

"He's taken an early lunch."

"I hope he eats something. He's lost loads of weight." I don't care. Stop caring. None of this is your problem.

"Haven't you noticed his clothes just hang on him?" Un-ironed and, more recently, unwashed.

"Don't you have some kind of duty of care to him?" Chris started at me blankly.

"All of this is stressing him out." I wondered if I should tell Chris about Neil's stressed induced OCD and germ

145

phobia. This manky old place would be the stuff of Neil's nightmares.

"What does he have to be stressed about? They've arrested someone." For Chris too that concluded the matter.

That seemed to be the only thing anyone cared about. I was alone in my obsession that the right person should find themselves behind bars.

The 'right person'. What did that even mean? That people get what they deserve? Life's not like that. I realised that a long time ago. Then, I'd been blinded by love. Duped into believing things could be different. Less than a year after my own little personal Armageddon it all felt very much the same. Ron wasn't just leaving for New York. He was leaving me. There comes a point in every relationship where you have to decide to commit or not. Ron had bought the ring and that reality had shattered the illusion. We weren't forever. We were just for now. It was all coming to an end.

"What are you looking for?" Chris, like Neil, was rummaging through the soggy paperwork.

I tried to distract myself with the unimportant. I didn't want to look at the all-consuming thoughts filling my head. *Having a ring doesn't mean he's going to propose. If he was going to ask, he would have done so before leaving for New York.*

"Maybe I could help you find it."

I wasn't having much success in finding a job. I could give my time away for free. What the hell, I was already wasting my life.

"The CCTV was removed. The sprinklers were turned off. Even I don't know how to do that and I worked here!"

Chris raised an eyebrow as though that was only further evidence of what a terrible employee I had been. I knew that I hadn't. Not this time. I did a good job and I cared. I really cared.

"Look Jen," Chris growled. "Just go home."

And, for the first time in months, that wasn't where I wanted to be.

CHAPTER 25

I was still furious with Chris hours later. The anger seemed to have kicked the stomach flu at least. For the first time in weeks I looked and felt grand. I was still bloated but the nausea had passed. That was particularly devastating as there was no excuse to miss tonight's birthday celebration.

'Girls only'.

I'd never been alone with Caitlin. Except that time I'd brought the wrong child home from Nursery and, even then, that was mediated by the Police and Social Worker. I would have to be fashionably late to be assured there would be other human buffers to our interaction.

"Have a lovely evening." Ron hovered apologetically as I prepared for the 'festivities'. His case was packed and waiting at the door.

I'd tried on about a million outfits. All of them lying to me about the changing shape of my body. This must be the middle-aged spread…. And maybe those four donuts I had after the altercation at work. My former work. Whatever. I was definitely joining a gym on

Monday. I'd have lots of time. When Ron finally left I could get one of those revenge bodies. Mine. Not his. I tried to suck my stomach in.

"You look amazing." Ron stood behind me with his arms around my waist. I allowed myself to lean back, in silence and feel safe.

"It worries me how convincingly you lie." I threw a third dress aside. Any other night and I would have decided not to go but, that wasn't an option tonight. My invitation was in the guise of an olive branch.

"I could at least come with you to the airport." At least. I hadn't said out loud Ron hadn't invited me to New York.

"I couldn't bare it." Ron nuzzled my neck. "I don't think you could either."

I wanted to ask what he thought would be different from all the nights we now spent apart.

"Do you need me to look in on your flat?" I tried to be helpful.

Something passed across his face. He paused before he spoke. His throat gave an involuntary spasm. "It's fine. I'll have someone from Smiths do it."

An employee rather than a partner.

"You were going to clear your throat." I tried to sound casual as I threw another dress aside. That little tic was Ron's tell. Before I knew his business had underwritten my loan Ron would clear his throat whenever I talked of the Bookshop.

"I'm emotional."

149

He lied.

"Is Brian going?" The question more bitter and accusing than I'd intended.

"Jen." His voice exasperated. Conversations about Brian always led to an argument.

"I don't want to go. I don't want to have to be dealing with this and, I don't want to have to do it without you." He sounded sincere. I almost believed him. "You're the only thing that gets me though it."

I wanted to believe him.

Ron glanced at the clock. He would have to check-in soon. "I need you and Caitlin to take care of each other."

I laughed bitterly. "Have you told her that?"

I was confident Caitlin was eager to, 'take care of me'. Only, it was more of the gangster euphemism for bumping someone off.

"You'll have a nice time tonight." His voice lacked conviction again.

I was to sit and enjoy drinks and a meal when my partner flew across the world without me. The physical distance would only replicate the emotional space between us.

Tonight was Caitlin's master move but I'd no idea of the game plan. I was an emotional wreck; doubting everything. Even the present. Ok, especially the present. It was supposed to be a joke. What do you buy the woman who has everything and all that?

Caitlin would hate it. Possibly more than she hated me. Maybe I should just stick some cold hard cash in an envelope. Or a cyanide capsule with the words, 'eat me'.

Ron looked at me, thoughtfully. He wanted to say something. The thing that would change our lives forever. The thing I didn't want to hear. I knew that look. I had seen it before. What felt like a lifetime ago. I'd chosen not to see that same look on Stephen's face in the weeks before he left. I told myself I wasn't sure what it meant; but I did. That look meant we were over. I tried to ignore it then because I hoped it would all just go away. I was naïve. Sometimes when things change, they can't change back.

Perhaps that is why I had only just built up the courage to ask Ron what was happening at Smiths. I didn't want to hear a pathetic excuse for the time spent at work, in the study and away from me. I didn't want to know the problem was simply us.

"What is it?" I whispered. At least, if he dumps me here and now, I won't have to go to Caitlin's meal.

Please God, I'd rather go. I'd rather this not end.

"I ...." Ron started, then stopped. "I could get the later flight and drop you off."

That wasn't what he was going to say.

Ron knew I didn't want to go but as this was a Caitlin based interaction, very little could actually be said.

I straightened his tie and resisted the urge to cry. I didn't want to go to the party but, I didn't want to be here without him either. It was a dreadful reflection of my inner turmoil that I would rather be with Caitlin in a room filled with what I can only imagine were other carbon copy Caitlins than here. It was a poor indication for the future.

A few weeks. Ron said he would be gone a few weeks 'Working through the issues with people smarter than him.' They'd 'get to the nub of it' he assured me but, he hadn't sounded convincing.

Two weeks. If I was better at Maths I could work out how many hours, minutes and seconds that would be. All I can definitively say - too many.

"I'm going to miss you." Ron looked sad. Really sad. Sadder than someone should look who is only supposed to be going for ten days.

"I'm coming back, soon, and I promise you. I won't leave again. We'll be together forever." He tried to be flippant but, Ron knew as well as anyone, there's no such thing as forever.

CHAPTER 26

Either Caitlin and her clones had arrived early or she had told me to come late. They were all thin, blond, plucked to an inch of their life and possibly surgically enhanced. Still, a group of the most conventionally beautiful women I have ever seen. I knew I'd stand out. I just hadn't imagined it would be quite this much.

Caitlin smiled painfully when I arrived. Making it clear to all my presence was under duress. There was a garble of whispers and hushed voices: 'Quite chunky', 'not what I expected' and Caitlin's voice in the mix, 'she's really got complacent'. I pulled my handbag over my stomach. For all of life's little disasters Mother Nature's monthly visit was about to appear.

No Jen, not disasters. It's his job. He had to go.

Ron seemed genuinely torn about going. 'Let's just say, see you later.' He whispered as the taxi driver peeped the horn impatiently outside.

When things were really bad Mum had told me to think, 'I just need to get through the next 10 seconds.' Only, those small chunks of time led inevitably to Ron walking to the door. It started a series of events that led him to the airport and boarding a plane to New York.

I cried from the moment he left.

What is it about me that makes men want to leave? Maybe Ron had to go. But did he really have to go alone?

Caitlin didn't hug and kiss me when I arrived. She looked disdainfully at the gift bag. "Put it on the table."

With all the Jo Malone gift sets. Yup, the gift was a terrible idea.

"This is just supposed to be a joke." A present you have to explain tends not to be the best kind of present.

Caitlin looked suspiciously at the gift bag; as though it was about to detonate. That had been my first thought too. Maybe we had more in common than I'd thought.

The waiter approached. I'd like to say they have the sixth sense for those in need but this was yet another venue terrified it would be pulled under by a negative review. 'I had to wait a full eight seconds for a drink...'

"Can I get you a ... Jen!"

"Stephen!" Again!

Caitlin looked between Stephen and I. "You know each other?"

"We used to live together." I rushed to explain.

I wondered if Caitlin knew that. If Stephen being here was all just part of her malevolent plan.

Stephen wore the same shirt and trousers from the night before.

"Flatmates?" Caitlin wasn't going to let me off so easily.

"Actually, I was going to ask her to marry me," Stephen filled the glasses of water on the table.

I didn't know what to say. I never quite knew what Stephen was going to do. I'd thought Ron was going to ask me to marry him but his plane taxied down the run way four hours ago and he seemed particularly anxious to be on it. He didn't even want me to go with him to the airport.

'I couldn't bear to leave you behind' he'd whispered early this morning; the first time we had woken up together in months. Then he did. He physically left. He'd checked out mentally weeks ago.

I wanted to roll up into a ball and cry. Instead, I was about to be torn apart by a pack of hyenas. Or, those wild dogs at the zoo. The ones that have the sign above the enclosure stating, 'Whatever falls in here. We ain't getting it. Sunglasses, car keys, kids, whatever'. Sure, the pack looks beautiful but, it'll tear you to shreds in seconds

"Is this the one who ripped Daddy off?" Caitlin seemed genuinely angry but tried to mask her fury. "Or do you have a string of former lovers?"

It was tempting to admonish a grown woman for the use of the word 'Daddy' but I wasn't sure it was Caitlin I should be reacting to. Stephen's ludicrous idea that he was going to propose deserved to be challenged, didn't it?

Why do you care?
I don't.

You want this time with Ron to be different.

It is.

It isn't.

"I'm doing a couple of waiter jobs." Stephen smiled. "Twins."

Life's moving on for the entire planet.

Caitlin smiled nastily. "Its sweet. She knows the help. Drink up ladies." Caitlin turned her attention to the group before I could respond. "Craig's treat."

"I'll bring you something sweet, fizzy and incredibly alcoholic. Just how you like it." Stephen touched my arm, with something close to affection and camaraderie.

"Sorry." I mumbled. Not even sure that he heard it.

"Why are *you* apologizing to *him*?" Caitlin spat the words. "He's a criminal."

He was other things too.

Caitlin made me feel that in defending Stephen I had betrayed Ron. I wanted to say something about treating everyone with respect. I wanted to tell Caitlin to stick her party where the sun didn't shine but I couldn't bear to go home. The flat screamed Ron's absence more potently than when he locked himself in the spare room. So, I just sat down and said, nothing.

A little bit of me felt sad when Stephen walked away. As though I no longer belonged to his world, but to this one. *No Jen, you need a world of your own.* That's what Ron's giving us. Space. Only, Ron had put the distance between us before he even left.

"Amy." One of the blond bombshells smiled effortfully and held out a limp hand for me to shake. "I believe you're the wicked stepmother."

"They're not married," Caitlin laughed. Before adding, pointedly: "Dad's still grieving."

You'd have thought that little nugget would have killed the mood. There'd been little enough atmosphere when I arrived.

The clones spent the next few minutes exchanging meaningful glances.

My plan had been to keep quiet, fly under the radar and at least make a few of them question the bad press I'd been given. Then, I'd head home to an empty flat and an even emptier bed.

Maybe I should go back to my folks.

"It's weird," Amy who was drinking for three called out. "I used to sleep over all the time at your house. Caitlin, do you think old Ron had the hots for me too?"

Caitlin blushed.

"What is it you do?" Caitlin 2 smiled, sympathetically, to the Queen Bee as though her attempt at conversation with me was the ultimate demonstration of loyalty.

I didn't even have a job. It's not that I've ever even had a successful career. I wasn't really trained to do anything.

"Jen's unemployed," Caitlin sneered.

"It's not as simple as that." I protested. Although maybe it was.

Caitlin 2 winked. "No point in having a dog and barking yourself."

Further insinuation I was only with Ron for his money.

"She worked in that dodgy Community Centre that burned down." Caitlin beamed. As though the demise of the Centre was further evidence against my credibility.

Maybe it was her who lit the fire.

"Wasn't someone stabbed there a few months back?" Caitlin 4 looked horrified.

"Yeah, but I'd given them ample warming not to piss me off. Hormones ladies, am I right?"

The group of, I don't know what you'd call a bunch of Caitlin's, crows had stolen a murder so maybe a nightmare, the nightmare of Caitlin's, paused, briefly, as some tumbleweed blew past our table.

These were not friends who discussed hormones or, anything that was actually meaningful. Maybe I was being unfair. Perhaps the hype I had been given by Caitlin enabled them all to believe I really was capable of stabbing someone. In which case I was useful to know; this lot would want people dead. They just wouldn't want to get their hands dirty.

"What are you doing for your actual birthday?" Caitlin 3 asked.

It may have been an attempt to relieve some of the awkwardness from the situation. It served more to underline that this wasn't the A group. No one here was important enough for the real birthday celebrations.

"Well," Caitlin looked almost petulant. "With Daddy in New York"

I'm not sure how *that* can be considered my fault.

"Craig's taking me to Paris."

I wanted to ask about the carbon footprint that had seemed all consuming when the St. Rapheal trip was abandoned.

"Flying?" I raised an eyebrow.

"Isn't Craig good?" Caitlin 2 beamed. "And babysitting tonight."

"Does he have other children with him?" Parents loved to talk about their kids. That could be my in.

"He's looking after Joey." Caitlin snapped.

I was confused. "Isn't that just parenting?"

Caitlin flashed an eternity ring at the gaggle of magpies. A shiny distraction from the inadequacies of her husband.

I smiled and nodded too, trying to remember how many times I had actually met Craig. Not that I was complaining. Craig was a little bit handsy.

"See" Caitlin thrust the diamond encrusted eternity ring under my nose. "It's from Tiffany's."

It was from Ron. The ring was for her.

159

CHAPTER 27

They'd spent most of the evening discussing the highlights of Paris. The best places to eat, to drink and to shop. They'd complained about the food, the service, the cocktails, the location of the table. Our evening had been punctuated by an apologetic Stephen. Caitlin was punishing him for knowing me. I could have said something. I tried to, but I couldn't think what to say. I was spending all my energy trying not to cry.

The ring had been for Caitlin.

A game of top trumps as to who was the most cultured was going on around me. They all lost. All were dickheads and I couldn't help but feeling like I was the biggest one.

Why was I here? If I was to stay with Ron this would be my life, and even if he was to tolerate Caitlin hating me, would I?

Why am I saying if?

Ron and I weren't ready for marriage. My heart almost stopped when I thought he was going to propose. When Ron said he had something he wanted to ask me

– I told him not to. So, why was I upset the ring had been for Caitlin?

"Tell them that funny thing you told me, Jen." Caitlin's voice boomed across the table. It felt like the whole world turned to look.

I can't recall Caitlin ever enjoying a story I'd told.

"The time I collected the wrong child from Nursery because you told me his duck trousers were one offs and…"

There was a mass gasp.

"About going on a bus to Paris." She interjected, more annoyed than usual.

"It was a school trip."

They all laughed hysterically.

"What kind of school did you go to?" Caitlin 3 mocked.

"A good one." I bit back. "It was reformed."

A moment of tiny revolt.

"You weren't interested in a trip to New York?" Caitlin 2 slurred.

Cailtin held her finger to her lips. "Not asked." As though it was a secret. Then, they all fell about laughing again.

I wondered if this was what Ron had anticipated when he asked Caitlin and I took care of each other.

"Well, that makes the next question almost moot." Caitlin 3 gave away how much of the evening they had planned.

Caitlin 4, looked directly at the ring leader. "So." She elongated the word and turned her attention to me "Are you and Ron planning on tying the knot?"

Stephen had awkwardly appeared to mop up a drink one of them had knocked over. His presence was an unexpected bonus. Although I suspected Caitlin had banged the table to make sure he was here for this latest performance.

Caitlin pretended to dramatically choke on the seventeenth glass of chardonnay she was chugging back.

"Sorry," she giggled. "Don't tease her."

"Tease?" I shouldn't be playing this game. Caitlin couldn't have known I'd found the ring. The assumptions I'd made.

Caitlin put her drink down, enjoying the attention of the crowd, savouring the moment she looked me straight in the eye.

"Sorry Jen, I was only thinking of you." She spoke loudly to drown out all other conversations. "I mean, it's all just a bit of fun isn't it?"

"No." I mean, it's fun. Well it was, but it's way more than that. I never believed in soul mates or any of that other greetings card crap until I met Ron.

Ron's age didn't matter. His wealth and status didn't matter either. I told myself in time, neither would Caitlin.

'Richer than Midas.' Chris words echoed in my head. 'In case you don't know that didn't turn out well.'

How would I know how that story turned out? Apparently I went to a terrible school. Evidenced by the fact we travelled to Paris on a bus. I thought there were league tables for school performance measures but there you go, wrong again.

"Oh." Mock horror spread across Caitlin's face. "I thought you understood." She turned to Caitlin number 4. "He never lets her stay in our flat."

Speaking about me as though I was some animal not allowed on the furniture. She paused dramatically. "He's never quite got over the death of my mother but he's a man." Caitlin waved her hand dismissively. "Jen isn't the first 'little distraction'." She retuned her attention to me. "And she won't be the last. Ask him about his personal trainer."

CHAPTER 28

It hadn't been my finest moment. Knocking over my drink and storming out of the restaurant. They'd have a field day with that. Even as I left I heard it: 'Well, you were right about her.' Caitlin would already be on the phone to Daddy. His plane would just have landed.

My phone buzzed into action.

"Jen? What happened?" Ron's voice anxious on the other end of the phone. "Caitlin said you ruined her party."

The party was ruined the minute she arrived. That was before I even got there. That woman was in bad company when alone.

"Why do we never stay at your flat?"

Silence.

"What?" Ron stalled for time.

"You heard me."

"Jen." Ron stumbled for words he couldn't find or mustn't say.

"When was the last time you came with me to visit my parents? I'm dragged along to incessant meals with

Caitlin and, what, you can't spend half an hour having coffee with my parents?" I could feel anger and resentment building in me. "You see how she treats me and not only do you let it happen, you allow it."

So do you.

"And what about your personal trainer?" I'd brushed it aside. He was supposed to go three times a week but last week I'd read a text message on his phone saying he'd missed two appointments. I'd laughed and given up on the couch to 5k App for another week. Where was he going when he should have been at the gym? He left with his bag. He wanted me to believe that's where he was headed.

"Are you going to answer me?" People in the street were looking. I'd become the delulu woman crying on the phone to her boyfriend. Strangers in the street knew what Ron was doing when he was supposed to be at the gym.

"I'm coming home."

"And where's that, Ron?" The line was cracking. He was fading away.

"You keep some stuff at mine and we pretend that we live together but, you're rarely with me now." I could feel the anger building. No longer just at Caitlin but also at Ron.

"Relationship." I spat the word. The months of pent up anger started to overflow. "What kind of relationship is this? I don't even know why you had to go to New York."

You didn't want to know. He could see it. You wanted him just to tell you it was all ok.

"Jen …. Talk …. Future…." His phone crackled. The miles between us more evident.

I could hear Ron was in a car. Driving from the airport and further from me.

I hung up. More shocked than anyone that I'd done it.

Ron was one of the few people I always picked up the phone to. Anytime. Any place. And, I'd just hung up. Not because of Caitlin but because of him. Caitlin was right. We never stayed at Ron's place. His flat wasn't part of an old life. He still went there; two or three times a week. Picking up post, watering plants and paying reverence to some kind of mausoleum. I never went with him. That was where he escaped from me. Goodness knows what else happened there, or with whom. I'd been trying to ignore the warning signs. They were screaming at me now.

Ron tried to call back. I didn't want to speak.

He texted.

I didn't respond.

Caitlin was right. This wasn't forever. This was only for now. Ron told me he loved me. He touched me, held me and kissed me but, always behind closed doors. Hidden away in shower cubicles on the pretence of romance because he was ashamed. People thought I was his daughter.

'Going to bed.' I texted. Throwing my phone into my handbag. Ron was on the opposite side of the world trying to sort out a tiff between his children.

He'd been annoyed when he called. The day had come. Ron had finally taken a side. He'd expected more from me. He'd expected me to sit and take her crap. I wasn't the absent parent during her childhood. I shouldn't be picking up the tab for his mistakes.

Caitlin was still playing petty little mean girl games. Tonight the teacher had made me sit with the popular girls and they'd brought me down like a pack of passive aggressive lions. They'd not only torn me apart. They'd torn us apart.

CHAPTER 29

"What a bitch." Carol handed me a coffee. It was after midnight but she'd come as soon as I'd called.

"She was right." I whispered. Not wanting to acknowledge it, even to myself.

Carol shook her head. "She wasn't. She was trying to stir up shit and she has done. Call him."

I shook my head. "Of all the people who had to witness that, bloody Stephen."

"Stephen's an arsehole."

Stephen would be on the phone to his mother. Telling her how broken I am. What a lucky escape he'd had.

"He should be in prison. Writing his book." Carol sneered. "Caitlin would never have spoken to you like that in front of Ron and, if he was here, you'd have come home, fallen into his arms and it would all be ok."

Not this time. Not anymore.

"It's not going to be ok." Caitlin wouldn't have been as vitriolic if Ron had been there but, she hadn't exactly been reserved in front of him either. Ron had allowed this to continue. Perhaps there were other betrayals too.

"He's like a ghost. Ron doesn't live here. He just haunts the spare room."

Carol laughed. "Sorry, that was a bit funny."

There were glimpses of the man that I loved but mostly now, it was just some bloke who had the same face.

"He was mean about Stephen."

"Boo hoo." Carol poured herself a large scotch.

Ron's scotch. This place was littered with his stuff. I had nothing in his flat. Nothing. We stayed there one night months ago. I'd left my shampoo. He'd brought it back when he collected his post the next week. A bottle of shampoo; that I'd already replaced. Maybe it wasn't just that my super brain took everything in. Maybe it also filtered things out. Things I didn't want to see.

"Stephen ripped you off. We all say terrible things about him and he deserves it. Why do you hold Ron to a higher standard than the rest of us?"

I hated when Carol said obvious and sensible things. "He sounded like Caitlin."

"Ron would have been protecting you." Carol sighed. "Just like he always does."

"Not from Caitlin."

"Haven't we already covered that Caitlin a poisonous witch? I can't believe you checked his phone." Carol made it sound like a betrayal.

"I didn't. My battery was dead and he gave me his to order that nail polish I wanted."

"Well, unless he has a burner phone, I doubt he has a dark and terrible secret."

"No internet history." On the phone or the laptop.

I didn't tell her about the laptop.

Carol looked more serious. "Come on Jen, it's Ron. The love of your life. The man you said you trusted implicitly since the first time you met."

"He's lied before."

"That was different."

"Was it?" Ron could have told me he knew that I had been accused of fraud. He could have told me his company had underwritten my business loan.

"Lies of omission are still lies."

"You're being mental!" Carol had no concern for politically correct terminology.

"Am I? Or am I finally seeing the truth?"

Maybe I was like the fool in Shakespeare. The character everyone dismissed; the only one who really knew the truth.

Carol pushed the scotch towards me. "You need to speak to him." She looked at the clock. "It's like 8pm yesterday in New York. Call him."

I'd already turned off my mobile phone.

"Caitlin will have told him what an evil cow I am. I've played right into her hands." I kept forgetting which one of the pair I was supposed to be more angry with.

"Do you think he'll believe her?"

"Oh, he believed her."

I tried to knock back some scotch but ended up spitting it back out into the glass. It tasted more toxic than usual.

"I found a ring in his coat pocket. I thought …." I trailed off. "Caitlin was sporting it tonight. Claiming it was from her husband. I thought he was going to propose." I let a tear roll down my face.

"Craig?"

"No, I thought *Ron* was going to propose.

"Why did Caitlin claim the ring Ron gave her was from Craig?" Carol looked perplexed.

"I don't think that's the biggest question of the evening." Only, Carol was right. It was a good question I should that have asked – so much for the super brain.

Caitlin had told her nightmare that Craig was paying for the evening too. I knew it was Ron's credit card behind the bar.

Carol squeezed my hand. A modern woman wasn't supposed to admit marriage is what she wanted. I wasn't even sure it was. Only, when Ron didn't propose; it hurt.

"And where is he going when he's not at the gym?"

"You'll need to ask him." Carol rubbed my shoulders but, noticeably, she wasn't telling me to pull myself together.

"There's a hundred and one explanations. Maybe you just jumped on the affair bandwagon because you found out Stephen was already lining up your replacement

171

when you were still together. Don't let him and Dirty Di make you doubt Ron."

"He wasn't where he said he would be."

"And where do you go when you're 'running'?" Carol had bumped into me once in the park when I was reading *Screw You*; or one of the other publications designed to make us feel bad about our bodies, our relationships, and general existence. Apparently in addition to all my other life problems I'm supposed to be concerned about something called a 'hip dip'.

"That's not the point." Although, maybe it was.

Carol looked thoughtful. "What was the ring like?"

It had looked fairly innocuous in the Tiffany Box. Adorning Caitlin's finger it looked garish and grotesque. "Like something out of a Christmas cracker."

Carol laughed. "Then it clearly wasn't for you."

It never would be.

CHAPTER 30

I spent the night being angry with Caitlin, then Ron, and finally me. I'd built my life around a man before. The same one who watched it all fall apart earlier tonight. I vowed I wouldn't make that mistake again but, I'm destined never to learn. I told myself that it would be ok with Ron because this time it was different. I allowed myself to believe the lies.

"You all right love?" Mum handed me an iced bun. Carol had obviously put Mum on red alert and she'd 'popped in on the passing' first thing in the morning. There was nowhere in Mum's world she would go that 'passed' my place and certainly not at seven thirty in the morning. Suspiciously too Carol had hung around, making herself late for work, then Mum arrived about thirty seconds later looking as if she had just fallen out of bed.

"I bought you one of those expensive coffees you like, champ." Dad handed me a 'cost-a-lot coffee'. Close.

Dad was calling me champ. This was bad.

"Ron will be back soon." Mum tried to offer some kind of reassurance.

Ron returning home was just going to offer different problems. Our relationship was over. It had to be over.

"Carol said you'd had a tricky night." More concerned looks from Mum.

It had been a tricky night. Carol had stayed over. She slept next to me snoring like a foghorn.

I'd contemplated consobrinicide (killing a maternal cousin). I had looked that one up on Carol's phone. Mine was still in the drawer.

"Have you spoken to Ron?"

I wanted to call him. I wanted Ron to tell me it would all be fine but, he'd said that for months and it felt different now. Caitlin, never my number one fan, had stepped up her campaign of hate. The snide remarks were coming thick and fast. Increasingly in front of Ron and he let it happen. If I dared to protest it was all, 'she doesn't mean it'. But she did, and so much worse.

"He loves you." Mum reassured.

"Maybe not enough." I looked away. I didn't want my parents to see me broken again.

"You look tired, love." She ran her hand through my matted, greasy hair. "Things will look different after a good sleep and a wash."

Different. Not better.

I didn't go to bed until 6am and it was still the longest night ever. Whenever I slept I just kept waking up, reaching out and finding Ron gone.

What if Caitlin was right? What if Ron still loved his wife? Would I live in denial just to have him here, with me? Maybe it was enough that Ron made me happy. Only, this wasn't what happiness is supposed to feel like.

Ask him about the personal trainer.

Why did I keep forgetting Ron was supposed to be having an affair?

"You need another focus." Mum, ever the problem solver, was planning ahead. If Ron was going to leave I had to have something else to concentrate on. Something to get me through.

"Did you know Barbra's cat had kittens? We could get you one of them."

"Did you know Stephen was married?"

Mum looked at the floor.

"The gun is still smoking from that wedding." Dad had occupied himself fixing a squeaky hinge. That's what Dads do in a crisis. I hadn't called this Armageddon but the appearance of Dad and his toolbox was more of an omen than the four horsemen of the apocalypse.

"Stephen's moved on." I continued.

"I don't think it feels that way to him." Dad was suddenly very profound. "It doesn't look that way to the rest of us either."

Dad tended not to say much but, when he did, it was usually insightful. Or something about hinge brackets that no one understood.

It wasn't about Stephen. It shouldn't be about Stephen. Only, in marrying Dirty Di he had set that relationship apart from ours. My life was supposed to be different too. Only now, it felt very much the same. I felt the tears roll down my face. Ron was right, Ron was always right. It was a crappy time for him to leave.

CHAPTER 31

"Who were the mean girls?" Stephen appeared behind me at the self-service queue in the supermarket.

I was trying to contemplate if the machine was more or less judgy than the cashier. I tried to convince myself I was rocking the no make-up, dress-down chic. Rather than looking like I'd tried every drug on the planet. Mum and Dad had run out of little jobs and excuses to be at the flat. I had the bloody awful feeling that Mum was on her way to Barbra's to source me a kitten.

I think I'm allergic.

I've also always advocated that preferring cats to dogs is part of a sociopath check list. I may even have quipped that having a cat is a symbol that you've given up on life; you can't even commit to a dog.

I had told my parents I was going for a bath. I should have followed through on that plan.

"Off to the gym?" Stephen looked at my tracksuit bottoms and made a generous guess. This 'lounge wear' was one of the few things I could still fit into. Just as well,

I'd spent the past three days lounging. I probably smelt quite ripe.

I tried to recall if Stephen had seen me look worse. Once, when we were together, I had come down with flu. He'd stayed out all night with friends. Well, new work colleagues. Stephen didn't really have friends. Few people hung around him for long. Except me. I never learn. It only occurred to me now that Dirty Di could have been on that night out. I tried to feel something for her other than pity. One day, maybe that day has even come, she would be the sick partner at home while he's out enjoying life.

"The mean girls were Ron's daughter and her friends. She's not my number one fan." I had a disturbing image of Caitlin 'hobbling' me.

"They weren't fans of me either." Stephen retorted.

It was a painful reminder of how rude they had been to him too. How I had just stood by and watched it happen.

"Sorry I didn't speak out." There was no excusing it.

"You're not the one who should be apologizing." He looked embarrassed. "Especially to me."

Stephen was wrong about that too. He may be a dickhead, asshole and all the other things my family accuse him of, but I wasn't. At least, I was trying not to be.

Stephen picked up a newspaper. "At least we're not in New York. Three inches of snow apparently."

Ron was still in New York. The pictures in the newspaper another painful reminder of his absence.

"All the planes have been grounded." I heard that on the news.

Ron probably wasn't even trying to get home.

"I wanted to call you the other night and check you were ok." Stephen was holding a meal deal. Coke, tuna sandwich and crisps. It was a small relief that some things in life didn't change. I could have picked that lunch for him. Only, it was dark outside. Perhaps Stephen was nocturnal now. Like one of the vampires he'd written about…. Hang on, they were zombies. How could I have forgotten that?

"I must have hovered over your name in my phone about ten times since that night.. Do you still have the same number?"

I had changed my number twice since Stephen had it. "I lost my contract when…."

"Oh," Stephen looked embarrassed. "Sorry. Again."

The past would always hang between us. Stephen would forever be defined by the dreadful event.

"He put a good word in for me at the court case. Your new man. It helped. Probably what kept me out of jail. I'll be spending the next year in a high viz vest doing Community Service though." Glancing out the side of his eye, Stephen caught my gaze. I used to find that charming.

"I bet I'm the one left cleaning up Woodfield." He sighed. "Small world."

179

Maybe too small.

"It's hard getting any kind of decent job with a criminal record. I'd like to say the tips are good as a waiter but, I could never lie to you."

I wondered how Stephen categorised what he did. Wasn't it lying when, one day, he just left. Taking all my money, meaning my business had to fold in the same week my flat was repossessed. All the time having a question mark hanging over my head as to whether I was in on it. What Stephen did took planning. Perhaps he never lied but, he certainly withheld the truth.

"What are you up to these days?" Stephen tried to move the conversation on. Perhaps he realised too how ridiculous his last statement had been.

I hadn't even thought about a job in the past few days. I hadn't really thought about anything. I'd watched daytime TV and slept. I didn't even have the energy to go and harass Neil at the Community Centre. I hadn't even thought about the plight of poor, wrongfully imprisoned Mac.

I'd tried to call Ron a couple of times. Withholding my number. I was having trouble getting through. This was the longest we'd gone without speaking. This would be my new life. No more Ron. I would have to start describing myself as 'man free'. Employment and future free too.

"At least you have a job." Stephen knew I wasn't going to the gym. I wasn't going anywhere.

"I have several jobs." Stephen sighed and cast his eyes to the ground. A gesture of complete desperation. "You could have one of mine."

"You're popping up everywhere." I hadn't meant to sound so resentful.

I'd been the one to say I didn't want us to pass in the street. Only, I thought that time would be in about fifteen years when none of this would matter. I didn't think I had to add that I didn't want to be bumping into him every second day. Maybe it would always matter that he'd screwed me over. Maybe I'd never be comfortable around him now.

"I'm sorry I keep gate crashing your nights out." Stephen sounded almost apologetic.

I shook my head, well, I tried too. The nights out were ruined long before Stephen appeared.

"You seem to be living the high life."

That's how it could look from the outside. Expensive restaurants. Cards offered for payment without even looking at the bill. I knew it was a privileged position. Only, I knew something else too. I was miserable.

"Would it be weird to go for a coffee?"

He saw the hesitation.

"What about if we drink these cokes outside on the bench?"

CHAPTER 32

I didn't say yes. I didn't say anything but I found myself being herded outside and then sitting on the bench. I didn't have anything planned. Just a life stretching out in front of me, alone.

"You seem," Stephen paused. "Not yourself."

I wanted to say he didn't know me anymore. I wanted to be wildly different from the person he once knew but, I wasn't sure. The world was ending all around me and, again, I hadn't noticed until nothing and no one could stop it.

It had been kind of Stephen not to mention my running out of the restaurant, crying. Kind too to be compassionate about my dishevelled appearance. I had been more judgemental about his.

I hadn't been charged for offences against him though so, that was something.

"We spent a long time together." Stephen handed me the can of cola. "If I can help."

"Who said I needed help?"

No one needed to say it, Jen. It was evident.

Stephen looked awkward. "I owe you so much. I can't believe what I did to you. To us. Some kind of breakdown, I guess." Stephen looked genuinely shocked. As though he'd only just remembered or realised what he'd done.

"None of this feels like me. Do you ever get that feeling?" Stephen looked bemused by his own appearance.

Everyday.

"No."

I wasn't sure there was any of me left. I'd just allowed myself to be ushered out of the shop to the bench because I had no energy left to fight. I'd backed myself into this corner. Pretending Stephen and I could still be friends. Pretending I was ok his life continued when mine was imploding.

I was glad Stephen had recognised that woman in the restaurant with Caitlin and her friends wasn't me. I didn't belong in Caitlin's world. Maybe I didn't belong with Ron either. Perhaps, in the long run, it really would work out.

"I'm ok." The thing people say when they aren't.

"Things aren't great at Smiths." Stephen leaned back on the bench. "That has to put pressure on everyone."

Apparently the whole world knew.

"Can't be that bad though, with Mr. Smith footing the restaurant bill. That place isn't cheap."

It felt weird hearing Stephen be so formal about Ron. I suppose that's how we are supposed to address grown-ups.

"It was Ron's card!" I was glad I was right about something. There hadn't been a last minute change of plan. "Caitlin said her husband was picking up the bill."

"Cheap at half the price for some time away from that one." Stephen smirked.

"You should be glad you left when you did. Overpriced crap." Stephen laughed. "The blonde bitch was mortified when the card was declined."

"The card was declined?"

"He telephoned and used another card. No big deal. Poor bloke. He looked shattered when he came in earlier that day to the restaurant. You need to go easy on him, Jen."

It was odd hearing Stephen sympathise with Ron.

"More money, more problems, I guess." Although it looked like Stephen had enough problems of his own.

"I'd rather be crying in a Bentley than on a bus, right?" Stephen pulled out my trusted mantra.

"I'd rather not be crying at all." I couldn't understand why the card had been declined. Ron was so conscientious about paying bills on time and he always paid the credit card bill in full. Always. Perhaps the card issuer had tracked his location to New York and suspected fraud.

Other questions were beginning to emerge. Like, why did Caitlin tell the nightmare the ring was from

Craig? Or, lie about the 'one off' trousers that were, in fact, from a high street retailer. Not even a high end retailer. Those trousers were worn by every other child in the Nursery the day I collected Joey. Then, there was the hat. Caitlin was proud of her luscious blond hair. Why cover it up with that ridiculous hat?

For the same reason you did in High School, Jen. Roots! Caitlin the immaculate must have needed her hair done. She had proudly shown it off on her birthday.

"Why was the card declined?"

Stephen shrugged. "It happens all the time."

Not to Ron.

"They didn't seem like your crowd." Stephen smiled, sympathetically, although by the end of our relationship I realised much of my crowd had fallen away. For a time there had only been Stephen and I. Then, there was just me.

"Maybe you don't know me anymore." It sounded harsher than I had intended.

"Sorry, I'm holding you up."

Stephen always has a sixth sense for me pulling away. He wanted to get in there first. Another little victory. He would go home and tell his mother how kind he had been and they could all feel a bit less bad for upending my life.

"Ron's in New York." I don't know why I told him. Perhaps because at this moment there was no one left to tell.

Stephen nodded, as if he understood something I didn't.

I could see images of the snow-covered city in the headlines. I could have seen it first-hand only, well, Caitlin had comprehensively addressed why Ron hadn't asked me.

Maybe Ron was as ashamed of our relationship as she was. Maybe he too was lining up my replacement. An older woman. Someone with more sophistication, who'd wear a twin set and pearls. She'd talk about Chaucer and never think to ask at 3am whether penguins have knees. He'd laughed then, pulled me close and whispered, 'Go back to sleep. We'll find out tomorrow'. When I woke in the middle of the night more recently Ron was never there. Perhaps him leaving would not be so much of a change.

"He'll be snowed in." Stephen assumed he was trying to get back. "Worse places to be than New York." Although, like me, he had no way of knowing. Stephen and I had never travelled.

"I don't think he even recognised me that first night."

The night I didn't want to think of. The night I thought Ron was about to propose.

Stephen had brought Ron and I together. Ron had given a statement in court and, despite all that, he didn't recognise him. Ron hadn't even been looking.

"He's a bit preoccupied." The understatement of the year.

"Was he jealous?" Stephen nudged me, playfully. "You think he'd be jealous now?"

Stephen held my gaze and, it may have been my imagination, but a weird moment passed between us.

CHAPTER 33

I tried to stand up but Stephen grabbed my hand.

"I was joking, Jen." Only, he wasn't.

Stephen was doing what he always did; test the water.

"Jen, this isn't what I want." He pulled at the wedding ring with anger. "It's never been what I wanted. I wanted us to be together."

"Stephen, Stop. I thought we were…" I struggled for a word. Not friends. Friends was too inadequate for all that had passed between us. Perhaps there wasn't a word for what Stephen and I were now.

"Don't you think fate is trying to tell us something?" His voice was desperate. "The world keeps throwing us together."

The last meeting theory. I'd read about it online. As a chronic insomniac there wasn't much of the internet I hadn't read. The last meeting theory is the idea that when two people had fulfilled their purpose in each other's lives the universe will make sure they never meet again. Even if they live nearby and share mutual friends. Stephen and I had none of those connections and yet, here we were. Again.

"We have unfinished business." Stephen asserted.

"I have to go." I couldn't hear this. I didn't want to know.

"Why? He's not here. He's in New York. On the other side of the world. He did this to us, Jen. We hit a rough patch and he made sure there was no way back."

"He did that?" I shook my hand free. Stephen's touch felt like fire on my skin. It burnt.

"You were supposed to love me unconditionally." He sulked.

"Stephen, you ran off with all my money. The courts were coming after me. I lost my business, my flat...."

He put his head in his hands. "I would have fixed it."

"How?" I pleaded for the answer. If Stephen's Mum hadn't taken ill, if he hadn't come home I don't know how I would have fixed it.

"You said we could be friends." He accused; as though I was the one who had betrayed him.

"I said I didn't want us to hate each other." That was different.

"Don't go." Stephen looked up, his eyes wet with tears. "Don't leave it like this."

I wanted to run away. I wanted to be as far from Stephen and this place as I could be without turning back but, I had loved him; once. Maybe by constantly throwing Stephen in my path the universe was trying to show me where it all went wrong. Maybe I was supposed to learn something vital from this ghost of relationship past. Reluctantly, I sat back down to face up to whatever the universe wanted to show me.

Silence passed between us. Somewhere I heard a siren in the distance and a dog bark. The world around me felt empty.

"I think about you all the time." Stephen wiped a tear from his face.

"Don't look back. That's not the direction you're going." I nodded wisely. "It's something my friend Neil had on a calendar."

"I don't know a Neil."

Yeah, I'm not sure I do anymore either.

"How's the family?" I'd been thinking of his parents. The ones who'd concealed his whereabouts when he ran off with all my money. Not the wife he'd been lining up as our relationship breathed its last. Perhaps there were no safe grounds for conversation.

Stephen looked at his shoes. I remembered them. They would lie at the side of our bed. A bed we shared in the life we once had together.

"Sorry I was bragging about how well life was going."

Those shoes outlasted our relationship.

"I'm glad things are...." I was relieved when he interrupted. I didn't know what I was glad about.

"There's nothing to brag about." Stephen began fidgeting anxiously with his wedding ring. I had flashbacks to Caitlin's Christmas Cracker Red Herring.

"It wasn't planned. I was really drunk. By the time Diane claimed to know she was pregnant it was too late for...."

Claimed. He didn't believe her. He felt trapped. He looked it too.

There would be no writing philosophy, or desperately bad books about a zombie apocalypse, now. Not with twins on the way. I felt a rush of freedom and relief. For a few moments I could breathe easier. I had escaped that fate.

"We only got married because of pressure from the family. You know they were never happy about you and me just living together."

Just living together. He undermined our time together. Again. A time I'd hated. A time that I'd put behind me. Why did it bother me that he so easily dismissed it?

Because one day, Ron will move on too. One day you won't matter to him either.

"Alright with the fraud and theft charges though, were they?" I sounded bitter. I didn't want to be that person.

Stephen was broken. He sat with his head down, twirling his wedding ring around on his finger and wondering how the hell he'd got here. That could have been me. I could have been the one with twins due because when we were together life often just happened.

"I suppose it was always going to be weird seeing each other." My voice was softer now. Stephen and I had spent much of our adult lives together and then, suddenly, we were nothing.

"One stupid decision." Stephen caught my eye again.

"It wasn't just one." I held his gaze. "It was all the little decisions that led up to the one big one. Then, all the other moments you decided not to come back."

"It feels like it all happened to someone else. Like, I'm just watching it unfold. Do you know what I mean?"

Yes. "No."

A couple had been approaching. They paused, then changed direction. I looked rough. The type of person to be avoided on a dark night

"Who was that?" Stephen followed my gaze. "They look like they recognised you."

I didn't recognise me.

"What are you thinking?" A question Stephen rarely asked when we were together. I thought he knew me well enough that he never needed to ask. Perhaps he just never considered my thoughts. Perhaps he mistook mine for his.

"Just the future."

"What do you and the old fella have planned for his last remaining years?" Stephen attempted a good-natured smile.

"You know better than anyone what happens to plans." I smiled and stood up.

I didn't want to hate Stephen, but I didn't want to spend any more time here either. It was too painful. Maybe it always would be.

It felt wrong. Just sitting with him on a bench. We'd been close, once. We'd shared a life. A bed. We'd planned a future. We hadn't just drifted apart, we hadn't just fallen out of love. We didn't have any of the endings that could make this bearable. Stephen had committed a crime against me, and we had parted. There was nothing left to say.

"I wanted us to give things another go but Mum said she'd never seen you this happy. Apparently you were the talk of the place. Relationships are impossible to keep a secret."

His mother had kept other secrets; like the whereabouts of her son.

"You managed." Dirty Di was the kind of relationship you would keep a secret. Even when it stopped being shameful, on the 4th of Never. Maybe I was Ron's Dirty Di. I'd never believe that but I had to tell myself something to make the end of this relationship bearable.

"Diane swooped in after you'd gone. I was in pieces."

Just like that, Stephen was the victim again.

I didn't want him to finish. "I wasn't the one who left, Stephen. You ...." I trailed off. We both knew what he'd done. There was no need to say it. I wanted to leave Stephen as I had done once before, with my dignity intact.

193

"My parents thought it was my money too." Stephen tried to defend and deflect.

"The Police didn't." Decent human beings didn't.

"I didn't mean to hurt you." He tried again to take my hand.

"You didn't mean not to either." Our relationship was mostly about him. Perhaps that was why I was so angry with Ron. We were walking an all too familiar path.

"I have to go."

"Maybe the start of my marriage isn't ideal." Stephen had to convince himself there were better days ahead.

"What makes your relationship with him any different from ours?" Stephen saw no marriage as no commitment. Until last night I'd never doubted Ron's fidelity or his commitment. I didn't know if that was trust or naivety.

Stephen stood up too. He didn't want me to leave but he couldn't ask me to stay. "Don't you ever wonder what could have happened," he ventured cautiously.

"If you hadn't left me high and dry and at the mercy of the Police and bankruptcy courts?"

"If I hadn't made the biggest mistake of my life." Stephen held out his hand. He looked at the ring. "It should have been you. This should have been our life together."

I hadn't even realised I was shaking my head.

"We can make things right between us." Stephen pleaded. "We can be together."

"You'd leave your pregnant wife for me?" Perhaps I was supposed to be flattered rather than repulsed. I'd forgotten what a horrific human he could be.

"Diane shouldn't be my wife."

"And she knows that, does she?"

Stephen looked bitterly at the cheap gold band. "The whole world knows it."

He leaned in closer. We'd kissed before. We'd had sex before but, that was then. Now, even standing this close felt wrong. I backed away.

"Once she was pregnant." Stephen looked disgusted. "You know my parents. I've screwed my life up irreparably for the past few years. They made me live with the consequences."

This time.

They didn't make him come back from Brighton and confess to stealing all my money but apparently, a baby out of wedlock was the clincher.

It's hard to find words of consolation for the person who brought about my own little personal Armageddon. Harder still when they showed only fleeting remorse.

"You're not happy with him." Stephen had a glint in his eye. I'd forgotten how my unhappiness and failures could bring him pleasure. "You're not yourself."

I'm a better version of myself. At least, I was trying to be.

"It isn't love." Stephen laughed to hide the frustration. The process of getting what he wanted was taking too long. "He took your flat. Remember?"

"I lost my flat when you ran off with my business loan. Ron didn't even know me then."

"Still," Stephen smiled, "I suppose we all have a type."

"What does that even mean?"

Stephen walked away. His arrogance intact. "I think you'd better ask Mr. Perfect."

CHAPTER 34

Arsehole. Stephen is an arsehole.

So why was I pacing the flat? Why was I enraged that the only retort I could come up with was 'Takes one to know one'. It didn't even make sense!

I was supposed to love *him* unconditionally.

How was Stephen supposed to have treated me? Where did I disappear to in the relationship? When did I cease to have any rights?

I wanted to laugh.

I wanted to cry.

I wanted to scream with rage!

I was supposed to love him. Despite the theft, fraud and adultery. He was 'having a breakdown'. An explanation perhaps but, not an excuse. No thought about the impact of his actions on me.

Stephen was an asshole. Ron was nothing like him.

"We all have a type!" I threw the cushion from the sofa across the room. "A type!"

Of course Stephen was bitter. Of course he had to get a reaction from me. This was the first and only time he'd been made to face the consequences of his actions. His mother had all but exonerated his crimes. That period of time had been locked in a little box in her head never to be opened. Stephen expected all women to be the same. I had been the same.

For the duration of our relationship I had lived in the moment with Stephen or, I had been the grown-up. I had to be the bitch that said no. The one he complained about to others. He would elicit sympathy from others as he recounted by unreasonable reactions to bankrolling his dreams. I had lost track of all the little disrespects that led to the big one.

Stephen didn't know me. Not anymore.

Stephen's life was falling to crap. He just wanted to make me feel bad. Yet it infuriated me that he might know something I didn't!

"I think you'd better ask Mr. Perfect." I felt so angry I could scream, or throw up. I'd ditched the wine for another night. Drinking was a slippery slope. Even the smell of it made me nauseous.

I was going to have to phone the doctor tomorrow. I would have to waste precious NHS time and resources to be told what I already knew; I was beyond stressed. I was closer to breaking point now that I had ever been during Armageddon.

Ron held my hair and stroked my back when I first got sick. I wanted to cry at the warmth of his touch. I hated how even the thought of it calmed me.

Stephen always kept his distance when I was sick. Too bloody worried he'd catch whatever I had. Ron always cared more about my wellbeing than his. Whatever the secrets were, I had to keep faith. I had to believe he was trying to protect me.

CHAPTER 35

"I haven't seen you in days." Neil handed me a pint of milk as I opened the door.

I looked worse than he did that time he'd caught impetigo from that cat. I hadn't washed in two days. I still smelt faintly of vomit. Neil looked almost as bad. Even the milk looked like it had curdled in his presence.

"I thought I was annoying you hanging around."

I purposefully didn't invite him in. I'd get back to Daytime TV and the mundane life that stretched out in front of me.

"When did you stop doing things that annoyed me?" Neil tried to sound flippant but his face crumpled with grief. "I fucked up, Jen."

Ha! Neil had sworn. I had won the bet. Only, the victory felt hollow. Neil really did look like shit.

No, he's supposed to be your friend and he's lying. Or, at least, he's holding the truth back; the new kind of lying that everyone seems to think is acceptable.

Don't invite him in.

"Come in."

You see Jen, this is the problem. You just don't help yourself.

Neil picked up Ron's brandy. Good, drink the lot. One less memory of him.

Five days. I haven't seen or heard from him in five days. It's hard to keep faith when you're keeping it alone.

"The Mystery Man. Don't ask me who he is because I'm not telling you."

"Why aren't you telling me? Do I know him?"

Neil put his head in his hands and slumped onto the sofa. "He was there the night the Centre went on fire."

"Where?"

"At the Centre." Neil looked as though it was self-explanatory. "With me."

"What the hell were you doing there? Oh, never mind." I could see from his face what they'd been doing. "Why there?"

The Mystery Man was supposed to be loaded. A place of work was a really crappy date. Unless it was some kind of kink. Maybe the Mystery Man was one of those voyeurs. The kind who liked to read miserable books about kids who were sold for a packet of cigarettes. Real poverty porn stuff. The Community Centre would have been ideally located for that kind of perversity.

I know we're all supposed to be liberal and open minded. Goodness forbid we, 'kink shame'. Even when someone hurts others; even when they break the law and transgress the basic code of decency.

"You know the town has hotels."

201

Maybe Mystery man wasn't rich. Neil's smart watch could have come as part of a mobile phone upgrade deal or, the mystery man could have stolen it.

"Has the Mystery Man upgraded his phone contract recently?" I heard the hope in my voice. I wanted Neil not be involved with dangerous criminals.

"Jen, focus!" Neil pleaded.

"Why didn't you go to your place or, to his?" I knew the questions sounded like an accusation.

"I don't know."

That was the truth. I watched as Neil tried to make sense of what he was telling me. I saw the devastation in his face.

"I can't see why any of this matters. They've closed the investigation." I thought of Mac sitting alone, in a cell.

"Who told you that?"

No one had told me that. I just assumed.

Neil looked up, tears in his eyes. "I think he took the CCTV."

"Why would he take it? Were you being kinky?"

My mind raced. Neil was uptight enough to have a fetish.

"Are you one of those furries?" I managed a small laugh at the thought of Neil popping on a Mickey Mouse costume for sexual gratification.

"Aw, shit." My face contorted. "This isn't the kind of thing that's going to start trending on the internet, is it?"

Neil rubbed his eyes, trying hard not to cry.

I hesitated, but I had to ask. "Is it Mac?"

"No it wasn't bloody Mac." Neil looked up again, briefly. He had that same look. The one Ron had had. Stephen once had it too. Neil was about to tell me something that would change my world forever.

I waited. This time I didn't try to fill the silence. This time I needed to hear the revelation.

It never came.

"You could do worse than Mac." Not only had he been an electrical engineer he was a pretty decent bloke.

Neil couldn't make eye contact. "I think he took the CCTV because I think he's involved in the fire. In fact, I'm certain of it."

"You think Mystery Man burn the Centre down?" I laughed at the absurdity of it. "Was it an act of love?"

I saw Neil was serious.

"You can't go making allegations like that." This isn't like the time Neil thought he was an alcoholic because he was a bit lonely and wanted to go to the Club.

"Jen." His face darkened. "I am certain it was him. I confronted him later that night and he stank of petrol. That's what the Fire Investigation Officer said was used as an accelerant."

"Why, Neil?" My hours of binging crime dramas had taught me one thing. When people gave false statements they weren't always lying. Sometimes they had just become so invested in the case they convinced they felt they were part of it.

203

"If I told you why you'd know who."

"So, I do know him?"

It felt like a lifetime passed between us.

"Well, you don't need to tell me but you do need to tell the Police. An innocent man could go to jail."

"I can't." Neil looked horrified. "You can't either. Promise." I'd never heard Neil sound so desperate.

"What about Mac?"

It would be pointless me going to the Police. What would I say? Neil knows something that you don't know. He'd only deny it.

"Why are you implicating me in all of this?" I heard the anger and frustration in my voice. It was good to feel something other than the mind numbing pain of the past few days.

I hated Neil more in that moment that any other. He had evidence that proved Mac's innonence and he chose to do nothing with it.

"Maybe it wouldn't be so bad for Mac. He'd have a bed every night and access to some good rehabilitation programmes."

"Have you been reading the *Daily Mail* again? Meanwhile, back in the real world Mac's not going to a health spa, Neil. It's prison."

I folded my arms and leaned casually against the wall. "Why are you here? I'm not your priest. We're not even friends. All you're doing is dragging me into your drama."

Tears were streaming down Neil's face. He looked terrified. Shaken to his very core.

"I thought were friends."

Friends don't implicate each other in crimes.

"I'm Mac's friend too."

Perhaps not in the conventional sense but relationships, like people, were complex.

I could feel my heart beating in my chest, pounding in my ears.

"Why aren't you telling me who this mystery man is?"

"You'd hate me." Neil's voice cracked.

"I don't much like you now. Who is it?"

"He pursued me, ok. You have to understand that. I tried to resist him. I did resist him but, he was relentless and I was flattered. Clearly I was just some bloody pawn in this whole fucking charade but, I'm not going to prison."

"Who said anything about prison?"

"I don't have an alibi for the fire. I've been stitched up." Neil started drinking straight from the bottle. "They'll blame me."

"What can't you just say you were with him?" I had thought the investigation was concluded. It seems I had been wrong.

"No-one thinks you started the fire." My breath felt shallow. People assumed Mac had done it; they weren't looking for anyone else.

"Neil." I whispered. "Who is this man?"

"I was sucked in. Won't be the first. Won't be the last. I thought he was different. I thought I was different."

"Who is it?" My question more insistent, but my voice quieter still. For a second I wasn't even sure that I'd spoken.

Neil looked up. He leapt to his feet, crying as he ran to the door. "I can't. I should never have come. You're going to hate me."

CHAPTER 36

"David!" I'd mistakenly opened the door in my pyjamas.

It had been a rough week. At least I'd washed and changed. After Neil's little visit I felt like I needed it. He wouldn't answer my calls. He wouldn't tell me who the Mystery Man was. This was the kind of week that should have involved drinking into the small hours, waking up hung over and to unexpected gifts from my drunk Jen. Goodness knows why drunk Jen thought sober Jen needed an array of tea cosies in her life but, there you have it. I don't even drink tea. I think the plan was to wear them as hats. I blame next day delivery. Thank goodness for the stomach flu. I was saving a fortune.

"Hey!" David looked embarrassed. "Ron called and asked me to check in on you. He was worried."

"Brian busy was he?"

Brian would still be in New York.

"Brian's a dick." David moved into the hallway. "Would you want him in your home?"

It didn't feel like home.

"Can I come in?"

The flat was a tip. My outward environment was a reflection of my inward mental state.

"Do you want a coffee?" I led him through to the carnage and hoped he'd say no. The milk Neil had brought was probably yoghurt now.

"Nothing stronger?"

I cracked open a bottle of brandy Ron had been given as a gift. Something to be saved for a special occasion. Neil had taken the other cheaper bottle with him.

"Have you seen Neil lately?"

Twenty-four hours and he hadn't taken my calls. He'd read the WhatsApp messages so I knew he was ok. I'd regretted my 'If you're being held captive in the mystery man's basement let me know' winky face. I was trying to be light-hearted but, that's the kind of crap they read out in court. It's not so funny then. It wasn't particularly funny now.

"Ron said Caitlin's party had been challenging." David appeared eager to move the conversation on. And he chose this, far more awkward topic, to do so.

Why was he avoiding talking about Neil?

"Challenging? Isn't that just management speak for bloody disaster?"

"Don't shoot the messenger. I get enough of that crap at work." It appeared that the conditions at Smiths had not improved.

David shifted a pile of magazines I'd been crying over as I looked at all the happy couples thinking, 'that used to be us'. You know, the kind of emotional self-harming we all get a kick out of. I planned to scroll through my camera roll later. If I could work out how to log into the cloud.

David looked anxiously around the cesspit. "Maybe we should open a window."

Neither of us moved.

"Ron has been trying to get in touch."

"The battery in my phone died." I didn't want to see if Ron had called; it protected me against the eventuality that he hadn't.

"Charge it."

I couldn't tell Dave the phone was no longer in my possession. I had to stay strong. So I posted it to Carol's holiday home in Spain. Her neighbour was going to return it but, that would take another few days.

"He called your parents. They said you were fine." David could see that wasn't the case. His eyes scanned the chaos of my surroundings. None of this was fine.

"You have to call him."

I didn't *have* to do anything.

"I can't." It was taking all my strength not just to cry.

I thought of all the mean things Caitlin had said; how worthless I had felt.

"Why are you doing this to him?" David demonstrated misplaced loyalty to Ron. "Why are you doing this to you?" His voice was more compassion in his concern for me at least.

"You didn't hear all the mean things Cailtin said."

"Caitlin said he's having an affair. She told me to ask him about his personal trainer." Ron's gym bag sat in the hallway. A potent reminder of the suggested betrayal. "He's supposed to go three times a week but, he doesn't. Where does he go?"

"Where he always goes." Dave reasoned. "Work. I'm not defending Caitlin." Although it sounded like he was.

"She's worried about Ron. We're all worried about Ron."

"What is happening at Smiths?" Hamster, stand down. I needed to hear this.

"You should ask Ron."

"I'm not talking to Ron. That's why you're here. Keep up."

"He's been trying to get home." David sounded frustrated by that. "Thankfully, the weather has meant he had to stay put."

"Why thankfully?" When Dave knew of both our distress.

David took another large swig of brandy. I realised now it was only 11am.

"Are you OK, David?" I thought of the hundreds of reports I'd tipped in the shredder at Smiths. "Is any of this because I did such a bad job?"

"If only! This has nothing to do with your antics."

David looked at me again. He stood up and began to pace. I'd never seen him pace before. I'd pushed that man as far to the edge as a person can go without actually falling, because apparently that's my thing, and I'd never seen him pace.

"You can't do this to him, Jen. You're the only thing that has been holding him together."

No. That was wrong. It was the demise of our relationship that meant Ron was pulling them all apart.

"I tried to call him." I wasn't going to tell anyone that. I wasn't going to be seen as weak. "I didn't get through."

"The phones were out with the weather and the meetings are incessant. Try calling again."

David looked at the I-pad sitting under my coffee cup. "You could Skype him or something."

It would be too painful to look at him.

"We need Ron focussed in New York, Jen." There was a desperation to his voice,

David saw the rolled up blankets on the sofa.

I'd taken to sleeping in the living room. I told myself it was because I was so unwell. In reality it was so I could watch the TV when I woke up crying in the middle of the night. It wasn't just because I couldn't be around Ron's things. Last night, I had caught myself sniffing his jacket and crying. That was a low point.

"Jen, are you ok?"

"It's a bug I think. It'll pass." I knew that it wouldn't.

"Where's Janice?"

"I can show you how to use Skype." It was a futile offer from the man who ought to know how hard it was to teach me things I didn't want to learn.

"David, where's Janice?" It was a simple question.

211

He took another swig of Brandy and gave me a sideways glance. He stroked his unshaven face. "She's with Legal."

"Legal?"

David's clothes were wrinkled; as though he had been up all night. "Have you slept?"

"Slept?" He laughed, bitterly.

"David, what is the 'lot' that's 'going on' at Smiths?"

"Ron was adamant you don't get to know until its sorted." David took another large swig of Brandy. "It's not going to get fucking sorted."

I stood in the silence. I held all other thoughts at bay. I held David's eye contact.

"There's some, well, quite a few, financial irregularities."

"Financial irregularities?" I thought of the credit card that had been declined at Caitlin's nightmare gathering.

David sat down, then promptly stood back up.

"People could go to jail. It's serious. Really serious. Ron's all over it but the financial regulators are in. There's massive payouts on tiny buildings. It's bad Jen, it looks really bad for everyone."

"He never said." I mean, I switch off but I'd hear 'prison'. Even if I missed 'New York'.

He doesn't trust you. You shouldn't trust him.

"Ron doesn't want to implicate you." David respected Ron enough to come and check in on his cray cray girlfriend. Or maybe, just maybe, he respected me.

"Why would I be implicated?"

212

David looked anxious. "Ron's one of the people who could go to jail."

CHAPTER 37

Financial irregularities. Prison.

My head was spinning. I felt sick.

I was sick.

Twice.

"You knew!"

Carol shifted awkwardly in her chair. "Jen, the whole world knows."

I remembered Mum telling me even Dad had heard something and Dad hasn't known who the Prime Minister was since Tony Blair.

"How? How does the world know?"

"People talk, Jen. People who have investments, insurance and…"

"I get it." I held up my hand. "I get it."

Grown-ups. Grown-ups talk about grown-up things.

Carol had asked poor wee what's-her-face to 'hold her calls'. Wee what's-her-face had taken one look at me and tried to call security. It's great I could still embarrass my cousin as well as my boyfriend. Ex-boyfriend. How can I even think Ron and I are still together? How long does it take of ghosting someone before a relationship is officially over?

214

Stay focussed, Jen.

"You never said." It felt like Carol had been complicit in the secret.

"You are aware that we're not in a relationship, right?" Carol was rightly confused as to why my anger was directed at her.

I had to be angry at someone. I had to mask the disappointment in me.

Sisters before misters, or Mrs. in her case.

Carol tapped her nails against the sparkling glass table. Her office was sleek, clean and expensive; how things used to be at Smiths. No one would be cutting Danish pastry Friday here. Or charging £1 for cat piss coffee.

 "It wasn't my place to tell you. Ron clearly didn't want you involved but, if you read something other than trashy magazines."

My fault. Again. Carol had a pile of financial magazines on her desk.

"They look boring as hell. Give me the highlights."

"You need to call him. Now!"

I'd tried. Straight to voicemail.

I had to replace my phone. I said a silent prayer and thanked the Cloud (and the genius who restored them) as hundreds of messages from the past few days flooded my phone; all from Ron.

"He's probably living it large in Ecuador."

Carol laughed, "Or breaking it bad in the Middle East." She caught my eye. "Jen, you don't think he's guilty!"

"I didn't think it was possible Stephen would leave me high and dry."

"This is different!"

"Is it?" It all felt very much the same. "I've screwed it all up again."

Carol frowned. "Look, Jen. No matter how far you go down the wrong road you can always just turn back."

"You just read that off the calendar."

"You were the one who gave it to me!" I had. After Neil had given it to me.

"What does that even mean?"

She folded her arms and looked me straight in the eye. Carol waited a beat. She had to be sure she had my attention. This was important.

"It means you've been drowning for weeks and all I've heard you do is describe the water."

"I thought we were on a road."

The truth of her words hit home.

"What kind of partner am I? Too wrapped up in my own little bubble."

"That 'little bubble' involves keeping an innocent man out of jail. Let's not forget that." Carol objected. As though I too had a right to have been distracted.

"And how's that going? Wait, you believe me? You don't think Mac burnt the Centre down either."

"Of course I believe you." Carol leaned back in her chair. "You're slightly, what racist Gran would call 'touched', but you have good instincts, Jen. You're right about lots of things."

I wanted her to give evidence to back up her statement.

"You want to know why Alice hates you?"

"Alice hates me?"

"You say I don't care what people think of me but you're wrong. I care what a *few* people think. Your opinion is one I value. When you call I drop everything and, you might not have noticed, but I'm not the only one. I will deny this to the death if you ever tell anyone I said this but, I admire you. You care deeply for others and you stand up for injustice wherever you see it. Those are qualities that matter in the people we love and I mean love in the platonic sense, not the sense that drives Alice wild with jealousy."

"Alice is jealous of me?" That felt better than dislike.

"I think you're missing the point." Carol scowled.

"It's not helping Mac having me on his side." He was still in Police custody and from what I understood, Ron, David and Janice were all about to join him.

Carol folded her arms. "Yeah, well. It's not over yet."

217

CHAPTER 38

"Ron's been distracted. I've been lonely for weeks."

"Of course he's been distracted." Carol handed me a glass of sparkling water.

"There's a lot of people's lives on the line. Criminal charges too. The whole business would go under. That would mean more people losing their jobs and their homes. At the very least." Carol gave a little swivel on her chair. Undoubtedly, the highlight of her day.

"He didn't tell me."

"Plausible deniability." Carol tapped her perfectly manicured nails against the glass desk.

"Smart move. If it was me I wouldn't tell Alice either. I'd tell you though, make sure you drop that into conversation next time you see Alice. I would be more than happy to implicate you." She smiled.

"You just want to make sure we're cell mates."

"Screw that." Carol protested.

"You think he was protecting me?"

"Hasn't he always?" Her voice softened again.

"I don't need to be protected."

"This isn't a blow for feminism, Jen. This has nothing to do with gender politics. We protect the people we love. End of. You, in your own little warped way, do the same. You held back on ranting to him about Caitlin because she's his daughter and he loves her."

"And look how that worked out."

"I'm just pointing out that you both acted with the best of intentions but, now is the time to tell each other the truth. No matter how awful it is."

My mobile buzzed into action again. Unknown number. I hoped it was Ron and yet, I hesitated.

"Carol, do you think Ron might be gay?"

"Gay?" She almost fell of her chair.

"I had Neil around earlier."

"Neurotic Neil?" Carol clarified.

"I only know one Neil." I was tired of asking her not call Neil Neurotic. "He wanted to tell me something about that guy he's been seeing and today he was all, 'I can't tell you who it is. You'd hate me.'"

"You think it's Ron?" She laughed. "Jen, I really don't think he has the time."

Time. Is that all that would stop him?

"Who else could it be? Who else would he be seeing that I care about?"

Carol shrugged. "Your father?" She laughed.

"Jen, I'm joking. It's probably that Cretin Chris. You hate him. Actually, you hate a lot of people."

Carol sighed. "Besides, I thought you said Ron was having an affair with his personal trainer."

219

"No, I said that is where he should have been." One of the many reasons Ron had provided over the past few weeks not to be with me.

"So, he's gay now and having it away with Neil?"

"Yes, no. I don't know." Maybe Ron was with Neil when he should have been with his personal trainer.

The call had rung out. There was no message.

"What do you think?" I pressed Carol for an answer. I wondered if an affair was something people ever really moved past.

"I think you should talk to Ron."

I wanted Carol to say I was being ridiculous. The one time I needed her to say it; she didn't.

"Do you think love is unconditional?"

"Is this about bloody Stephen?" Carol's tone irate.

"Yes. No. Maybe."

Would I still love Ron if he'd betrayed me? Could I? Would I be able to make a rational decision to love him, or not? Or, would knowing the truth change how I felt about him?

"All love is conditional." Carol pulled her chair tighter under her desk. She folded her legs with grace and dignity. I wished I could be that composed if only for a moment.

"Stephen didn't want unconditional love. He wanted to shit on everyone and not be held accountable."

"Healthy relationships are based on mutual respect and you don't get that from shagging Dirty Di."

"What about Ron and Neil?"

220

Carol's face was unreadable.

My mobile buzzed again.

Carol looked at it pointedly. "You should get that."

I didn't want to answer it.

"Whoever that is really wants to speak to you." Carol evaded the question again.

Reluctantly I answered the call.

"Jennifer Blake?" The voice at the other end was anxious.

"Yes, who is this?" Six months since I was declared bankrupt and still cold calling gave me chills.

"This is Hopfield Hospital. We've just had Caitlin Smith admitted."

CHAPTER 39

I hated the smell of hospitals. The cold clinical corridors full of the sick and the dying. I was probably about to join them. I'd run all the way and burst into A & E in a panic.

A nurse led me to a side ward where Caitlin was lying on a trolley, doubled over in pain. Instinctively I rushed over and took her hand. She curled again into a ball, crying.

"I didn't think you'd come." She winced again with the pain, or from the shock of my touch.

"Of course I'd come." I stroked her limp, sweaty hair from her face. "What happened?"

"I don't know. I woke up this morning in agony and Craig…" She trailed off. "Dad's away and there was no one else." She screamed through the pain. "Literally no-one else."

"I know. I get it. I couldn't get in touch with your Dad either." *Your Dad*. I'd distanced him from me already. I looked around the room for a distraction.

"Where's the doctor?"

"On their way." Caitlin grimaced.

"Why did they bring you here?"

Caitlin was incessantly banging on about her private health care, same day treatment, lack of waiting lists blah, blah, blah.

"Why do you think they brought me here." Caitlin snapped. "No health insurance."

I tried to harden myself against her but, it was impossible to hate someone in this much pain.

"Can I get you a drink?" I sure as hell needed one.

Caitlin shook her head. "They said the morphine should kick in soon." Her body was slowly beginning to relax. " I just hope to God I'm not pregnant."

Another reason to hate her.

No, I didn't want a baby. I wasn't built for motherhood, remember. I didn't even like children. Particularly her child. Besides, I didn't want to be a single parent and I'd either be separated or have a man on the inside. At least then I could be sure of Ron's fidelity. Unless he was having an affair with Neil.

"It's ok." I assured. Although I had no way of knowing that. No way either of knowing what Caitlin wanted from life.

Her lip began to waver. The ice-maiden was going to melt. Well, at leak a bit at least.

"You're in the best place." Although I'd just seen a tramp pissing in a corridor. Maybe the politically correct term was homeless person but, I had no idea of his residential status.

"I'm being punished." Caitlin wept. Proper ugly crying.

"Don't worry about ...."

"Not for you. It was ...." Her sentences were punctuated by deep breathing. It looked like a strategy she had learnt during pregnancy. I hoped I was not about to be witness to a birth.

"Craig and I had been going through a difficult spell."

I didn't want to hear it. I couldn't hold any more of that family's secrets. I wasn't joining either of them in their sordid little lies.

"Maybe another child is just what you need." I've seen too many episodes of Jeremy Vile to really believe that.

"Craig's had a vasectomy."

Oh .... Oh!

"It was a one off. Craig was working long hours. I was stupid. It's just if Craig comes when the doctor is here and the doctor thinks ...." Caitlin was crying; howling.

"Things haven't been right for a long time. I don't know what to do but, this would make the decision for me."

I didn't want to help her. I wasn't going to help her. Caitlin was my enemy. She'd systematically tried to destroy and undermine me since we met. This was my chance. The day of the underdog. I could watch her entire life fall to pieces in front of me. Why not? She'd been complicit in destroying mine. Only, I couldn't. I wouldn't. When you've sunk to rock bottom you can't let anyone else fall that far. Not even her. Caitlin might be a dickhead but, I'm not. At least, I was trying not to be.

"If Craig comes I'll keep him busy."

Caitlin looked utterly bewildered. "You should tell him."

"I'm confused. Do you want me to tell him?"

Craig wasn't exactly a 'catch'. Neither of them were but, you take some consolation they weren't out in the world ruining two couples.

"Why are you being so nice?"

I was being how I had always been. "I won't tell Craig anything you don't want me to."

"I would tell if it was you."

"Good to know." I poured myself another drink of water. I hadn't been able to tolerate anything stronger in weeks.

"I told Dad you were seen the other night with the bell boy."

Stephen.

The use of the word bell boy was to affirm how well travelled Caitlin was in comparison. There were so many ways I fell short in her estimations.

"He took your hand." She accused.

"He tried to."

"Is that who you were meeting in the greasy spoon?"

The all night café.

"You weren't at your parents. He called them. So where were you? And, more importantly, who were you with?"

Ron knew that I had lied.

"How do you know any of this?" How did Ron.

"So, what has this all been about? The long game?" Caitlin growled assuming Stephen and I had always had some kind of masterplan.

"Have you spoken to your father?" Somehow her calls were getting through and she'd spat poison into his ears.

Caitlin had the demeanour of the person who was asking not answering the questions.

"Whatever you think it was you saw, or whatever it was you wanted to see."

"I didn't see anything. You and I are not the same species, Jen. I'm not trawling the streets at night. Especially those streets."

"Your Dad told you about cousin Lyz being a sex worker, then." Another reason to hate him.

Still, I couldn't.

"No!" Caitlin choked on the air.

The shadowy silhouettes flitted briefly through my mind. 'Who was that?' Stephen had asked. 'They looked like they recognised you.' Two of them. One larger than life and the other, smaller, but familiar.

"There's nothing going on between Stephen and I."

She laughed, bitterly. "That's exactly what Daddy said."

I could feel the tears sting the back of my eyes.

"He said there would be a reasonable explanation and you weren't having an affair. He wanted me to call in and check you were alright. He's been trying to get through." She laughed. "I told him to get some minion from the office to do it. David or the Jackie one."

"Janice."

"They all seem incredibly fond of you." Caitlin looked bitterly at her drip. "If you have been screwing around karma will catch up with you."

Caitlin tapped her morphine button again. It beeped, cutting off her supply.

I didn't want to think of it being me. I couldn't imagine myself being with anyone other than Ron. I finally understood why all my other relationships had failed. I couldn't put it into words. I only understood this one worked because it was meant to. Until the past few weeks I'd felt closer to Ron than anyone else in the world. In a few hours that was all gone. It couldn't hurt anymore that another dream was about to die.

"It's not going to be me. None of this. The affair, the pregnancy. Not that I'm judging you."

No Jen, don't tell her. She's the enemy. Take the moral high ground instead.

"I don't think I can have children."

We hadn't exactly been trying for a baby but we hadn't been trying very hard to prevent one either. There had a been a few peeing on the stick moments but our bodies knew what I was only just realising. Ron and I weren't compatible.

Caitlin looked as though she was about to sneer and then something close to compassion swept across her face.

"It might not be you." Her eyes lacked focus from the drugs.

I waited.

What the hell, she was high on morphine and probably wouldn't remember any of this.

"What do you mean 'it might not be you'?" There may have been a secret vasectomy or some veneral disease that had ravaged his reproductive system. A consequences of all his little 'distractions'.

"Mum got really pissed one night and told me she'd had loads of affairs." Caitlin slurred.

"I shouldn't be hearing this." Ron's relationship with Laura was sacred. Only, perhaps it was me that thought that. Ron rarely spoke about Laura and, when he did, only in connection with Caitlin but, they must have been happy; once.

So were you and Stephen.

Caitlin laughed bitterly. "Ron might not even be my Dad. So, there you go Jen. You win. He's all yours."

"Win?" I knocked the morphine button from her hand before she launched in for another dose.

"Even if that absurd little idea is true. Ron is still your Dad. He's the one you phoned when you were brought into hospital. He's the one you grew up with. Even if he never did get you that bloody Furby."

Caitlin glanced at me. For a heartbeat there was almost a connection.

"No one wins this. We all lose. Just by varying degrees. I had no intention of ever making Ron choose between us. That's why I put up with all your crap. For him. And, if you were ever to have made him choose, I'd have left. Ron loves you more than I'll ever understand."

I know love is supposed to be blind but in this case it would have to be deaf as well.

"That's why I didn't take his calls. You're birthday party brought it all to a head."

Caitlin looked horrified. As though she'd only finally realised what the whole world knew before her.

"You really do love him."

"Yes." I loved Ron. I had never forgotten or doubted that.

What about his personal trainer?

Loving someone means believing in them. Even when he's not here. Ron trusted me when Caitlin tried to convince him I'd been unfaithful. Without hesitation or question. But trusting him when he'd given me so much to doubt? Was that love, stupidity or a bit of both?

I could feel the dreaded hormones kicking in my lady parts. Maybe I should have one of the medics take a look at me too.

"As neat a little ending this would be if you weren't his daughter." I stroked the hair away from her face. "You have his eyes. You have no idea how hard it is to see so much hatred looking back from them."

Caitlin lurched forward in pain.

"Given the circumstances," I handed her back her morphine button. "Let's just call a truce."

She looked back at me with Ron's eyes and nodded.

CHAPTER 40

I should have asked Ron what was happening at Smiths. In my defence, I had. He just didn't answer. Or, at least, he didn't provide a coherent answer. There was a lot of disturbance on the line. I couldn't hear him. Part of me wondered if I wanted to.

"That bus boy was shagging around when you two were together?" I'd seen American sitcoms and knew she was referring again to Stephen.

"It happens. No one needs to get hurt." Caitlin dismissed.

"And yet." I gestured to the hospital room and morphine drip.

"I don't want to share your father with someone else."

I wouldn't. I couldn't.

"Not even for his money?"

"I'm not interested in his money."

Caitlin rolled her eyes. "Well, that checks out. Even before all the rumours about the business you two didn't exactly live the high life."

Cailtin looked at me. As though seeing me for the first time. "He's proper ancient." She almost laughed.

"Not to me."

I didn't owe Caitlin an explanation.

"It's like that story from Plato's Symposium."

"Plato?" She laughed again. "Are you shitting me?"

"The god Zeus split all humans in two. Our quest on this earth is to find our other half."

"And that's my father, is it?" She sneered.

I had thought so.

"You Dad is like the ying to my yang." I knew I was mixing my philosophies now. "He makes me more serious and I bring out the silly in him." At least, I used to.

For a second Caitlin looked almost moved.

"He worries about the age difference." Her voice sounded different. Less sing-song and rehearsed. Almost human.

"Is there someone else?" I felt weak for asking. "Someone older, who shares his interests and has heard of half of the bands he tries to talk to me about?"

Not that Ron spoke about music much these days. He didn't speak about anything.

"No-one's heard of those bands." Caitlin smiled.

I'd accepted the image of Ron as a distraught widower, perhaps because it suited me. There must have been others.

"He's been distant."

"Dad's not shagging around." Caitlin blurted. "He's been overwhelmed at work, trying to protect you from how bad it all is and, I haven't helped."

As though admitting defeat, Caitlin continued. "I didn't tell him about Stephen either. Brian did."

"Brian?"

"Dad's twatty assistant. He saw you. He told me when I stopped into the office to collect Joey's red tractor. He left it when we brought Daddy lunch a few weeks ago."

Sure, Caitlin got past the Bull dog. "And you believed him?"

Of course she believed him. Caitlin wanted to think the worst of me.

"Brian was worried Dad wasn't taking it seriously enough."

"It was a chance meeting." Too many chance meetings. The universe kept throwing Stephen in my way.

"It wasn't just Brian that saw you. That fat guy from your work saw the pair of you too."

It was him that recognised you. Brian couldn't pick you out from a crowd."

"Chris isn't actually that fat. Wait. How does Brian know Chris?"

The shadowy figure at the door of the café. That couldn't have been Brian, could it?

Caitlin shrugged. "They used to work together. That's how I get access to Dad." She tapped her nose, well she tried to, but with all the morphine she missed.

"I keep their dirty little secret."

"What secret?

"Brian and Chris are doing the deed."

"What deed?"

"The sex." She whispered loudly.

'The sex'? Sure they are.

Brian and Chris. I almost laughed. She'd be seeing unicorns next.

"What about the personal trainer?" I shouldn't have asked. It made me look desperate.

Now wasn't the time to ask whether she thought her father was gay. Probably.

"His arthritis has been giving him hell. He doesn't want you to see him as an old man." Caitlin relaxed further in the bed. "He's obsessed with you. I can't see why but, he'd never betray you. I'm ...." It felt like the words stuck in her throat. "I'm sorry that I led you to think that he did."

"You're sorry?"

Caitlin had just apologised and the world didn't spin off its axis and go crashing into the sun. Nothing much had changed. I'd expected to feel better hearing her confess she was wrong but, the heavy weight stuck fast in my chest.

I should have been faithful to Ron. I should never have doubted him.

CHAPTER 41

"I didn't know you wanted kids."

There was much Caitlin didn't know about me.

"I just wish I hadn't eaten all the others." I tried to be flippant but the mood had changed between us. There was less animosity now.

Craig and Ron were still nowhere to be found. Caitlin's voice was laden with sarcasm and criticism. Or was that just her natural tone?

"I don't know if I do." Anymore.

I was much younger than Ron but I was no longer young.

"I don't think I'd make a good mother. Remember the incident?"

"I only made an issue of that because I hate you. I've done worse. I left Joey on the bus once." Caitlin laughed. "And I never told anyone," she whispered, now sucking on gas and air, "because I didn't want anyone to know I was on a bus."

There was a bit of an awkward silence.

I remembered the so-called designer baby trousers that were bought from a cheap high street fast fashion chain. The eternity ring Caitlin claimed Craig had given her and the pretence that her husband paid for her birthday meal. It only just occurred to me too that as Caitlin was here, she wasn't in Paris. She wasn't even with Craig.

"Caitlin, why were you on the bus?"

"The same reason I've been wearing that bloody hat for weeks." Her eyes filled again with tears. "You're going to love this."

"You don't have to tell me." Maybe it wasn't right to extort information out of someone this high on drugs.

"Craig's business isn't doing well."

Craig's businesses were never doing well. Craig had the kind of business ideas that were so bad they could only be a front for money laundering. I often wondered how long it would take Craig to contact Ron and ask him to back a book on a zombie apocalypse.

Caitlin fidgeted awkwardly with the eternity ring. Her hands looked smaller, more vulnerable.

"Craig asked Daddy for money and, he said no."

"He said no?" I couldn't quite process it.

Ron was like a blank cheque to Caitlin and Craig.

"I didn't know how bad things were until the credit card was declined at the restaurant." Caitlin looked distraught. "That's not true. I didn't want to know but, I at least, had an inkling. You were blissfully unaware."

"It wasn't blissful."

I wondered if Ron had any idea of the secrets I imagined he was keeping.

"You must have noticed the trips to the theatre dried up."

I noticed. I was just too grateful to question it. The opera had been amazing The post-modern interpretive dance far less so.

"The lawyers are good. But they're not cheap."

Caitlin pulled her hair forward. "See the roots? That's why I've been wearing a hat." Mousy brown hair sprang from Caitlin's scalp and bled into her perfect blonde.

"I assumed it was ombre. Isn't that all the rage?" I smiled, gently brushing the hair away from her face. The nurse had said they managed to get a hold of Craig. That was at least half an hour ago.

"You always look amazing."

Caitlin's face filled with appreciation. She was a bitch. Probably few people ever said anything nice to her. A compliment from me must have meant something; Caitlin knew that I hated her.

"Craig's left me." Caitlin glanced at me. She wanted to check if I'd revel in her misfortune.

"I'm sorry." Although I wasn't entirely sure that I was. Craig was a dick.

"Daddy said the whole thing at Smiths was a storm in a tea cup but, he's never said no to a loan before."

They'd never paid the money back either.

"I've been taking the bus, dying my own hair."

"Welcome to my world." The world that most of us lived in.

"The new outfit I had for the party, I kept the tags on so I could return it. It's bad at Smiths Jen, isn't it?"

That may have been the first time Caitlin said my name.

Caitlin wiped away a tear. "The whispers follow me down the street."

"I don't think it's a storm in a tea cup." From what I heard it was probably the end of Smiths.

"Craig just left. As soon as the money dried up. You and I have something in common. Isn't that what Simon did to you?"

"Stephen." I corrected, not that it mattered.

"I don't think I'll be very good at being poor."

"You get used to it."

Caitlin gave a wry smile.

"Do you really think that's why Craig left? Because Ron wouldn't help out?" It was hard to believe anyone could be so callous.

"I think there were lots of reasons."

CHAPTER 42

"A grumbling appendix." The doctor smiled.

Made sense. Every other part of Caitlin was bleeding miserable.

The appendicitis was nothing to smile about but high-on-drugs Caitlin was actually quite endearing.

I'd imagined a whole host of horrific consequences. I was relieved Caitlin was going to be ok. I should have been relieved we were to be spared a little alien gnawing its way out of her stomach; that's probably how she was spawned. Her and the little devil child.

Ron never said his wife had an affair. Several affairs if Caitlin is to be believed.

Maybe he didn't know.

Maybe it was just another secret he thought he was protecting me from.

Craig dashed into the room smelling of perfume. I noticed the shimmer of lipstick on his skin.

"Craig!" Caitlin beamed. "Great news. I have a grumbling appendix and I'm not."

"Anything more serious." I interrupted taking Caitlin's hand to silence her. Unbelievably Cailtin squeezed my hand. She was grateful that I'd stopped her. Sometimes that's what we need; for someone just to stop us.

Caitlin looked at Craig, disappointedly, "Thank you for coming."

The word eventually hung in the air between us all.

The separation was supposed to have been a trial and, whatever else Caitlin was, she was the mother of Craig's child.

"We'll need to operate." The doctor ploughed on. We'd all forgotten she was there. "You'll have to stay in tonight and we'll need some consent forms signed." She looked at Craig. Caitlin was six clicks of the morphine button beyond giving informed consent.

I'd thought Ron was like an appendix when I tried to leave him once before. Something you didn't really need but, I was wrong.

"An operation?"

I want to say that Craig sounded concerned. At best, he sounded inconvenienced.

"We need to remove the appendix." The doctor spoke as though it was the logical conclusion.

"You can't just do that!" I protested. "You can't just throw it away."

I actually said that. Out loud. To a doctor.

Everyone looked at me.

"I just mean, it hasn't really been any trouble until now. Maybe there's a good reason for all of this. Maybe we just have to find out what it is."

The doctor looked concerned. As though she was about to buzz someone from the psychiatric ward and have them assess me.

"Better safe than sorry." She settled on the path of far less paper work.

"You can't live life like that." I wouldn't it go.

"Pulling out at the first sign of danger. Just because you might get hurt or because you've sort of convinced yourself it might be gay and maybe a bit of an arsonist." I'd only just realised that little implication.

"Life involves risk. Love involves risk."

"Indeed." The doctor checked her watch. "Who's an arsonist?"

It would be nearing the end of her shift. "My medical training was hard so I'd rather not 'risk' it. If you don't mind I'll make the decision rather than Google."

There was no need to diss Google.

"You're not seriously suggesting that Caitlin keeps her appendix?" Craig looked horrified.

"Of course not." I'd sort of forgotten about Caitlin.

"I see what you mean." Craig whispered to his wife.

He tried to divide the sisterhood, but we'd moved past that. Holding her hair back as she'd vomited had created the sacred bond. Forged in fire and united over the one thing that had previously divided us; Ron.

Caitlin anxiously preened herself. She needed to look her best for Craig at this, the worst moment of her life.

I wanted to slap him. I wanted to scream I knew where he'd been; at least, I knew what he'd been doing.

241

Calmly, and with as much passive aggression as I could muster, I stepped forward and wiped the lipstick from his cheek.

"You've something on your face."

"Jen has been a star." Caitlin announced.

I waited for the sting in the tail.

Unqualified praise.

Wow.

"She's had a lot of drugs." I explained to the confused Craig.

Caitlin rubbed my stomach. "You'll make a great Mum."

Craig, slightly less concerned about Caitlin's plight, glanced at his watch. "Someone needs to pick up Joey."

Why were they both looking at me?

CHAPTER 43

To say the nursery staff were apprehensive about releasing Joey into my care would be a massive understatement. Three code words, four calls to Craig and the signing of a massive waiver sealed the deal.

At least Brandon was pleased to see me.

I had planned on nipping into the pharmacy but the security staff would be suspicious seeing me with another child. Caitlin had looked at my stomach when she smiled, 'You'll make a good mum.' Probably being a bitch. Implying I had child-bearing hips. Only I'd been blaming the demon hormones for weeks now and I couldn't remember the last time I'd had a period.

Relax Jen, it's more likely to be the menopause, or a hardboiled egg.

I wasn't sure I wanted to be a parent. Not now this little gift of creation had just thrown a dog shit at another child in the park.

Joey looked at me with his grey, blue eyes. Caitlin's eyes. Ron's eyes. Passed down through the generations.

"Where Mummy mad lady?"

I mean, I didn't love that term of endearment but it was better than grandma.

I got down to Joey's level, like you see adults do in all the books.

"Mummy has a sore tummy. So I'm going to look after you. Ok?"

Craig had said he would stay with Caitlin at the hospital. If you ask me he got the easy end of the deal.

Joey looked uncertain. I'd sounded uncertain. This past week I'd struggled to keep myself alive, never mind a small child.

Children are amazingly resilient. That's what the experts say on TV. Joey had little interest in Caitlin's whereabouts after that. Probably the 3½ years of close motherly contact was more than enough.

I didn't have time to think of a child care plan. That was fairly evident to all those around. The dog turd incident was the highlight of the trip to the park. He'd tried to kick a squirrel, head butted (let's say accidentally) another child and deposited a used nappy from a nearby bin into a 'yummy mummy's' Kurt Geiger handbag. My adult assessment of the situation was that it was time to move on. Joey had other ideas.

"You're not my mummy!" He hollered so the world could hear.

Strangers were turning around. One woman reached for her phone.

"Shush!" I have never felt more like the Child Catcher in my life.

"What do you want to do?" Super Nanny would be ashamed.

I was supposed to be in charge and setting firm boundaries. I'd Googled that on the way to Moonbeams.

Super Nanny could piss off. I wasn't having another almost child abduction charge to my name. Once is a misunderstanding. Twice is a pattern.

Joey nodded, testing the non-existent boundary. "Can we get ice-cream?"

If only my relationship with Caitlin could have been as uncomplicated. A quick ice-cream, tying of his shoes laces and Joey thought I was a legend.

It really helped I'd let him jump on our bed when we got home. My bed. Whatever.

We watched kids TV on Netflix until he literally crashed out on the floor. I hadn't really thought what to do beyond that.

I tucked him in the dishevelled bed and lay down beside him. Watching him sleep. Like some kind of lunatic.

CHAPTER 44

I wouldn't say parenting was a breeze. By 8am Joey had squirted toothpaste all over the wall and had a quick chew on the home pregnancy test I'd found hidden in an old handbag. Once he'd used it to stir my coffee of course. That was £2.99 down the drain. I'd need to start appreciating the value of money when my old man was on the inside. I tried not to think about Smiths for the millionth time as I threw the pregnancy test in the bin. I couldn't be pregnant. That was just a little mental breakdown. My classic Jen tactic for dealing with stress. Obsess about something unrelated and insignificant. There was enough drama without me inventing more. Yesterday I'd convinced myself Ron was gay.

"We're going to granddad's now." I tried to convince Joey of the need to wear pants.

My heart sank at the thought of walking into that flat. It felt like snooping. Caitlin had asked me to take Joey there. A quick keyhole surgery later and the hospital were happy to discharge her. Ron's flat was nearby. It made sense. She wasn't necessarily being an evil cow.

"My house." Joey sped around the flat like a whirling dervish. I was right - this kid was probably possessed. I should have dispensed with Super Nanny and called a priest.

"Grandad's." I picked up the spare key.

"My house!" Joey stomped his foot more adamantly.

The chocolatey breakfast cereal was probably a mistake but he'd looked at me with borderline contempt when I'd offered him a banana.

"Whatever." Caitlin could have that argument later.

"Mummy's going to be there. Let's get her some flowers."

Joey insisted on carrying the flowers. Then dead heading them by dragging them across the railings next to the park.

I'd had to fish him out of two bins. I hadn't even seen him climb in. I had finally met someone more impulsive than me.

By 1pm it felt like we'd visited every pet shop and swing park in the city. He seemed more energised as we turned into Ron's street.

"My house. My new house." He began dancing around further decimating the flowers, which now looked like some kind of threat.

I contemplated just buzzing him into the block and running for the hills. Only, Joey was too small to just leave at the door. I had to hand him over; if only to confirm I had the right one.

Joey ran and keyed in the correct four-digit code to open the door. Great, a three-year-old knows the code and I have to bring a key. This is probably where they meet and have lovely family time. Without me. I'd never be part of them. I repressed the familiar feeling of resentment

"Come on, crazy lady." His deranged little face smiled as he held out a sticky hand.

Joey's hands were always sticky. I knew that and yet, I still took it.

Joey rushed up the stairs. He burst in the door. "Cocoa!"

A black cat caught sight of him and legged it under the sofa.

I wish I'd thought of that this morning. Hang on, Ron has a cat?

"Joseph!" Caitlin reached out her arms and he ran into them. The two were genuinely pleased to see each other. I don't know why that should surprise me.

Caitlin smothered him with kisses. It was such a warm moment I felt like I was intruding.

"I'll just." I didn't know what to say.

I turned to go.

"Hang on." Caitlin stood up, awkwardly. "Will you please stay for a coffee?"

CHAPTER 45

I surveyed the chaotic flat I had thought was Ron's shrine to the past.

"Sorry." Caitlin looked frazzled. "I haven't had time to clean up."

There was a thing on Facebook about cleaning up when you had kids is like brushing your teeth while eating cake. With Joey it was more like brushing your teeth whilst simultaneously knocking them out with a toffee hammer.

"I didn't want anyone to know I was living here." Caitlin looked embarrassed as she handed me a coffee.

My first instinct was to sniff it but I had been fairly vigilant in watching her make it.

"Craig and I haven't really been getting on and I thought some time apart would help."

"I'm not just anyone."

Not my circus, not my monkeys.

I'd covered for Caitlin when I thought she might be at death's door. She's fine now. Well, not exactly fine. Caitlin looked almost translucent without make-up. She had dark circles around her eyes as she struggled to make the coffee. I could see she was in pain.

"Sit down." I encouraged.

It felt like Caitlin would resist merely because I had been to the one to suggest it but, she didn't have the energy, or apparently even the will, to fight.

"Why couldn't Craig move out?"

It was none of my business. Neither Ron or Caitlin wanted me to know this.

"We're having to sell the house." Caitlin looked at the floor, ashamed. "I did say Craig's business is not doing well."

"Ron wouldn't let you lose the house." I protested.

"He can't stop it."

I suddenly realised the wider impact of all that was happening at Smiths.

"It's not that Dad doesn't want you here." Caitlin looked around the flat.

Dad. The affectation of Daddy and the sing-song voice gone.

"He doesn't belong here anymore. This place is stale." Joey ran past throwing an action man in the air.

"Well, it was." She smiled. "I'm sorry about how awful I was to you at the party. When you left I opened the birthday gift. Everyone laughed. I wanted to cry. You remembered."

It was a one-off conversation. On one of the many guilt trips about how Ron hadn't been there for Caitlin as a child. He was supposed to have bought her a Furby on some business trip and claimed it had been taken from him at Customs. Caitlin resented it to this day. I'd found one on E-bay. It was demonic. The perfect gift.

"When my ex ran off and left me bankrupt he took this signed copy of *The Hitchhikers Guide to the Galaxy*. It was my prized possession. I bored everyone with how much it meant to me, how much it hurt me that he took that and when I finally got it back, I realised it was never about the book."

"Everyone else got me meaningless generic gift sets." Caitlin looked embarrassed. Reluctant to show further weakness.

"I called them. Before you."

I had been aware I would not be first on the list.

She waved her hand dismissively. "They were busy. It doesn't matter."

Of course it mattered. She was alone, and afraid.

"It meant a lot that you remembered. It meant a lot too that despite, how did you say it, 'all my crap', you came to the hospital."

I had hoped she'd have been too high to remember much of our conversation from the hospital.

"Not getting a furby didn't ruin your childhood or your idea of Ron as a father. I did that."

I was only a few years older than Caitlin. That had to be weird.

"You bring out the best in each other." Caitlin acknowledged. "He's happy. Less focussed on work. At least, he was, before all of this."

Caitlin winced.

"Still in pain?"

She looked at the bag of painkillers placed on counter top. I moved them to the top of the microwave; well out of Joey's reach.

"Where is Craig now?"

"He has an important business meeting."

This was important.

Caitlin's eyes filled with tears. "I treated you worse than I have ever treated anyone. Why did you help me?"

"Because I could." I had been to the depths of despair where Caitlin had found herself. I knew what it was like to feel alone.

"You looked worried. Really worried." She tried to understand the events of the past few hours. "Like you cared."

"I do care."

I cared about anything that was important to Ron.

Caitlin still wanted to hate me. As a faceless destroyer of a childhood that was easy but as a paid-up member of the sisterhood it was proving much more challenging.

CHAPTER 46

Caitlin was still feeling pretty crappy so I'd hung around to help contain Joey. Where's a straightjacket or some kind of tranquilizer dart when you need it?

I envied Joey. I couldn't recall a time I had so much energy, enthusiasm for life or thirst for knowledge. His most recent scientific endeavour had ended with melting two batman figurines in the oven. As a responsible adult I should have an inspiring monologue about fire safety. I should have opened a few windows mid-flow in case of toxic fumes. Instead, I'd spent the past ten minutes wondering what the plural of Batman is. Time well spent.

The flat was finally quiet, peaceful and still. Joey had collapsed in a heap on the floor. Face covered in jam. At least it would take away the taste of wee. Maybe I should fess up about the chewing on the pee stick incident. Only, things were going reasonably well with Caitlin. But, if Joey grew up as some kind of sexual deviant it would all be my fault.

I'd just have to live with it.

You won't know. You won't see it.

I didn't really know the protocol for this. Caitlin had crashed out on the sofa watching Ghostbusters. I had the bleak realisation I was probably now the responsible adult. Caitlin had taken a more hardcore painkillers. Lucky Caitlin. If Joey woke up he would need someone to be there for him. I grabbed a magazine and sat down quietly on the sofa. Being quiet wasn't exactly my thing.

My stomach churned.

I needed to practice being on my own. Maybe I'd go to India and find myself. Or go on a silent retreat. Unplug myself from the Matrix.

Ok Jen, you could start with putting Candy Crush away.

This was supposed to be the new me. Only, new Jen felt very much like the old one.

I wouldn't want to watch Ron leave. I couldn't.

Stop it! No one is leaving.

I leafed through the magazine again looking for a distraction. Finance, interest rates and a whole load of concepts that meant nothing to me. Carol was right. I should be taking an interest in the world around me. A proper grown-up would know this stuff. They'd have based their decision on which mortgage provider to choose on more than, 'this one gives you a free pen'. I'd lost that pen within a week.

Maybe that's why I'd fallen in love with Ron. I hadn't wanted a boyfriend. I wanted another parent.

I threw the magazine aside and flicked the TV channels with the sound on mute. A holiday programme.

I should travel. Then next time I'm mocked for going to Paris on a bus by Caitlin.

There won't be a next time. This is over.

Travel brings its own problems. Tapeworms. I'm not so desperate to be a mother I'd harbour a parasite. Although, it might be really effective for weight loss.

A Life insurance advert. Good. Ironic but, I could sort out a will.

Focus Jen. There was something my brain wanted me to see.

I flicked the channel again. A quick Google search told me I had none of the things I needed to write a will; the first being an idea of whom I would bequeath my worldly goods to. I wondered if Mum had managed to convince Barbra to give me that kitten; Tiddles could make out like a bandit in my last will and testimony.

I flicked the channel again. I should have stuck with Ghostbusters but it felt like there were enough spirits here.

Jeremy Vile. Maybe I should sleep with a long-lost sibling.

I turned the TV off. I wasn't looking for the next big adventure. I'd found it in Ron. Like a true professional, I'd screwed that up too. I'd got angry at him when Caitlin was rude to me. I believed the crap she fed me because every other relationship had ended badly. I couldn't just be happy. I couldn't just be in the moment. I'd made myself ill for weeks.

Very admirable Jen, but that's not it.

255

I picked up the magazine again.
A picture of an ATM.
It's not important.
It is.

CHAPTER 47

I stood up and closed the window. Darkness was falling and a cool breeze filled the empty flat. I adjusted Caitlin's blanket, contemplating waking her up. Ron's sofa was style over comfort. She'd wake up with a hell of a pain in her neck.

You're not supposed to care. Stop caring.

I scooped Joey up and took him through to what was Ron's study.

"The dinosaur's eating the cat. "He groaned sleepily.

Kids are bonkers. Maybe that's why I wanted one so badly. Joey understood how my mind worked. Only, one day he'd outgrow me too.

I leaned against the door frame watching him sleep. Anxiously checking his chest rise and fall. I genuinely never realised I could care so much about this pair beyond their connection to Ron.

Caitlin was right; I had been worried when I received the call. I ran to the hospital. When Craig arrived he just looked inconvenienced.

So much had happened in the past few hours. I needed time to stop and think. As per usual my mind wouldn't settle. Thoughts were buzzing around my head too quickly for me to focus on any particular one. Why was that picture of the ATM bugging me?

'He reminds me of you as a child.' Mum had smiled fondly as Joey head-butted a goat at the petting zoo three months before. We had been trying to be one big family then. I thought Ron had given up. I realised now he just ran out of time. The business and Caitlin's marriage fell apart and poor Ron was powerless to help either. Still, poor Ron could have tagged me in on this one. I could have at least not made his plight worse by endlessly banging on about the demise of the Leisure Centre.

The picture of the ATM flashed again in my brain.

I'm going to download a Mindfulness App. I'm going to try and work on staying focussed.

Only, perhaps the stakes were too high to allow my brain to focus. The brain protects us from the things we're not ready to see. I wasn't ready to face the consequences of all these events.

It was hard to believe anyone thought Ron was too old for me. I felt like I'd been dug up from the Garden of Eden, handed a coffee and set about my daily business. I'd been exhausted for weeks.

Mum thought Joey and I had the same 'zest for life'. I wonder if the doctors would advise he take medication; knock that spirit right out of him. Or, to 'help him focus'. I wonder what advice I'd give him. 'Quirky' is endearing as a child but tiresome in an adult. Maybe this wasn't about Ron, or Stephen. Maybe this has always been about me.

It's not that either, Jen. That's not the revelation.

Joey yawned. "I love you, crazy lady." Then he whacked me in the face with a tiny toy dinosaur.

I never seriously considered that I wanted children until it was becoming increasingly apparent that I couldn't. I watched the relief and love flood Caitlin's face when she saw Joey safe and happy. A tiny little part of me cried. I wanted more than a baby. I wanted Ron's baby. Watching this precious little angel sleep (I'd have never called him that two hours ago, or at half six this morning when he stuck his creepy wee face in mine), I finally understood. I let the tears roll down my face unchecked, unashamed as I realised my little world had just imploded again.

CHAPTER 48

The floorboards creaked. I tried not to notice. Ghosts lived in these walls.

They creaked again and an arm slipped around my waist. Ron held me close. There was nothing left to say.

"You're not supposed to be here." I finally whispered into the darkness. Not wanting to turn around and break the spell.

"I'm exactly where I'm supposed to be." He kissed my neck. "I'm so sorry about everything. I've missed you so much." His voice sounded fraught with emotion. There was a crack in his tone too; as if he would cry. I wouldn't look. I couldn't.

"It's ok." I found the strength to turn around to face him and my problems head on. "I understand now. He's so perfect."

Ron looked at the jam now congealed into Joey's hair and bedding.

"You and Caitlin have this whole other life together." I looked pointedly around the flat that had been adapted as their home.

"She asked me not to tell anyone."

"I sort of hoped I wasn't just anyone." My stomach churned, no bumped again.

I brushed my hand complaisantly over it. I'd see a doctor Monday. They'd tell me it was all just stress.

"I'm sorry." Ron placed his head against mine. "I was caught in an impossible position between the two women I love."

I wanted to ask him if he meant Caitlin. If there was someone else.

"I know." I stroked my hand against the side of his face. He looked exhausted. This was exhausting. I could feel the tears sting the back of my eyes.

"I'm going to make this really easy." I tried to be brave and noble. "We had a good run, right? Longer than anyone expected."

Just, perhaps, not as long as either one of us would have liked.

Ron looked horrified. I tried to move passed him but he wouldn't let me.

"Jen, you can't be serious!"

"Caitlin could have more painkillers at seven. You can only take so many in 24 hours. I'm sure you'll work it out. Make sure she eats something when she wakes up. We can talk in a few days."

We can talk about the practicalities of pulling our lives apart.

"A few days!" Ron stepped in front of me. "Like Hell we will. We haven't spoken in days already!"

There were tears in his eyes. "I tried to call. I sent David. I even asked Caitlin to go. This is all such a bloody mess. I was in meetings constantly and I can't fix it, Jen. I can't fix any of it."

I was glad the room was dark. I didn't want to see the tears roll down his face. Somehow the worst thing about all of this was Ron crying.

"I didn't come back for Caitlin. Well, obviously I would have done if I'd known, but the minute you hung up on me I jumped on a plane but they were all grounded because of the bloody weather. I came back here for you because maybe, maybe I can fix this." Ron looked anxiously around him.

"I wanted to do this in Pulling the Plug, the bathroom store that had been Hype. Remember?"

"When the manager kicked us out because he thought I was a prostitute. I've a vague recollection."

I knew then, I should have listened to that inner voice; our relationship was at the end. I tried to focus on what he was saying. Just get it over with. But I had a Proclaimers song going around in my head. What a time to get an ear worm.

He reached into his pocket and pulled out a little box.

"I swear to all that is scared if that's a key to this place I'm going to stab you in the eye with it."

I hadn't meant to say that out loud.

Too little. Too late.

Ron got down on bended knee. I saw a flash of pain; his arthritis.

"You'd better have dropped something."

I was being noble. History books would tell of the sacrifice I'd made in letting him go.

Ron popped open the box. I wasn't going to look. I'd be distracted by the shiny thing and unable to make a clear, rationale decision.

"What about Caitlin?" I protested.

Hoping, dreading that would pull him back to reality. He'd snap the silly wee box shut and we'd forget all about this.

"She's my daughter. I think the courts would forbid it."

"Stop it." I tried to be angry. I tried to resist.

"Jen Blake" I made the fatal mistake of looking right into his eyes. "Will you marry me?"

CHAPTER 49

I didn't say yes.

I didn't say anything.

Joey sat up, rubbing his wee eyes, "Grandad?" His face lit up and instinctively he reached out his arms.

Ron lifted him from his bed. Nuzzling into that jammy face. Joey hadn't even eaten jam today. It's like his body made its own.

Joey saw me and smiled. "Here you go crazy lady".

Joey plonked the pregnancy stick right into my hand. Two blue lines.

Ron looked from the stick to me.

"Caitlin's pregnant?" His eyes widened.

Someone sure as hell is.

"Oh my God." I dropped the stick. "He was playing in some bins earlier. Someone pissed on that." I ran off to the bathroom to scrub my hands with bleach.

Joey had his new word for the day ('pissed') and I learned an important thing about child development. It's impossible to ask a three-year-old where he picked up a pregnancy stick.

There'd been a few minutes in the park this morning when, distracted by a hoard of puppies, I'd seconds later found him in the trash; again. Joey had a habit of putting little treats in his pockets to be discovered later. I'd explained this to Ron and he'd smiled. 'You said you weren't good with kids. He loves the bins.'

'Please don't tell Caitlin.'

Ron kept looking at Caitlin expectantly, protectively. She was still his baby. Ron would remember Caitlin before she was battered by life and a bit obnoxious. Still, pretty creepy given he thinks she might be knocked up.

Ron looked anxious about being a grandfather again. He wouldn't want to be a father. Who'd want to get up in the middle of the night and change nappies. Hell, given the age difference I could be changing his nappy soon.

Only, another moment had been lost in the day. The one when Joey was eating his cereal. I had nipped into the bathroom too take a pregnancy test. It was just for peace of mind. So, I could focus on the rest of the day. Joey had begun slamming the cupboard doors and I didn't have time to check the result. I tried to remember the brand. I tried to ascertain if the stick Joey had just produced might be mine.

I poured myself a large scotch and then remembered I might be pickling my offspring.

This is absurd Jen, you're fixating. Deal with the real problems rather than the ones you've invented.

I handed Ron the drink. "Thanks." He looked confused. Probably because he was already holding one.

"I just remembered I'm giving it up for Lent."

"It's February."

"I carried it over."

Ron turned his attention to me.

I grabbed the scotch back. "What the hell, I'll start tomorrow."

I took a large slug and promptly spat it in the plant pot when he wasn't looking.

Caitlin caught my eye. "What the ...?" She mouthed, but with a child in the vicinity the latter part is not appropriate to repeat. Even though he was still stomping around the hall shouting "pissed" at the top of his voice.

"You don't like Scotch." Ron looked at me more intensely.

"You don't know everything about me." I tried to think of something I hadn't shared.

"Like, did you know I could have been a world class darts player, only I got the yips when I was fifteen?"

Ha! That would throw him off the trail.

Ron took my hand. Reluctant to let me go. As reluctant as I was to leave. He looked again anxiously towards Caitlin.

"I'm going to let you two catch up." I reached for my bag.

"You can't leave." Ron protested. "Five days, Jen." His voice pleaded. "Five days."

Caitlin coughed, discretely. I was almost impressed she knew how to be discrete but, then I was impressed to be seeing a different side to her.

"You haven't had dinner yet either. I was going to phone for a pizza." She waved a coupon. "I have a deal."

Caitlin had a coupon. That was even bigger news.

"Please," she caught my eye. Her request sincere. "Stay."

CHAPTER 50

"I didn't know Caitlin and Craig were still sleeping together."

Poor naive Ron. Maybe he didn't know about all his wife's alleged affairs. I wanted Caitlin never to have told me that. Knowing it felt like I had betrayed him too. It added to my guilt.

"I worry about the boundaries you have with your daughter."

"And when your mother made reference to my stamina she was talking about my golfing, was she?"

"Who knows what she's talking about half the time." I dismissed.

Ron hadn't golfed in ages. He'd gone to work early and come home late. Even at weekends.

You didn't want to see it. You didn't want to acknowledge the distance.

"I think he pulled that pregnancy test out a bin in the park. Craig's had a vasectomy."

"How do you know that?"

"Everyone knows that." Nicely deflected, Jen.

"Who puts pregnancy tests in random park bins?"

"Someone who doesn't want anyone to know they've taken a test I expect."

"Thank you." Ron pulled me in closer. "Thank you for being there for Caitlin when I couldn't. It's moments like these that make you realise what's important."

I think if he mentioned footnotes again I might cry.

"You're right." Ron looked guilty to the closed door. "I give her too much leniency."

"I don't need you fighting my battles." I admonished Ron for the very thing I'd wanted him to do; speak up for me.

"I should have set better boundaries." I asserted.

That almost sounded mature.

"I can't believe that shitbag just left her." I glanced too at the door. I lowered my voice. "He was with someone else when the hospital called."

Bastard.

"Sadly, that doesn't surprise me."

Perhaps Ron knew adulterers well.

"You didn't answer my question earlier."

Ron and I were in the spare bedroom. Caitlin and Joey were curled up on the sofa, watching TV, waiting for the pizza to arrive.

I hadn't planned to stay. I'd had so many conflicting thoughts and now he was here, standing in front of me. My Ron. Not some confidence philandering trickster. The man who held my hair back when I had stomach flu and told me I was beautiful, even when I didn't feel it. Especially when I didn't look it.

269

"Are you planning the wedding before or after you go to jail?"

I should have just said yes. That surprised even me.

Ron looked to the floor.

"You should have told me." I was trying to be angry but he looked exhausted. I think the disappointment in my voice hurt more.

"Which part?" He floundered at the magnitude of it all.

"All of it." I waved my arms round, pointing to the flat. "Caitlin's lived here for months."

"I'm sorry."

It wasn't enough. It would never be enough.

"I thought it would all blow over and I could tell you when I was the hero of the story. But I kept sinking deeper and deeper." His eyes were filling with tears.

I didn't want him to cry. I'd never seen him cry. It had been hidden by the darkness earlier.

"You are the only thing that has kept me going. Knowing you were in the next room gave me the energy to plough on."

All the nights I had felt isolation and despair Ron had felt only comfort.

"I know that was selfish. I could see I was losing you." He reached out and took my hand. As though to check I was still there.

"I could feel it and I couldn't stop it."

"You could have told me what was going on! This isn't the dark ages. I don't need to be protected. If there was distance growing between us it was you that was putting it there."

"I see that now." Ron sat down on the bed. The weight of his motion drew me there too.

"If I admitted it all to you then I'd have to admit it to myself and, I wasn't ready to do that."

Ron looked at the picture of him and Laura I'd removed from the drawer of his study on the one occasion that we'd stayed over. I thought he'd put it there because of me. I wasn't sure now.

"I'm so used to being the one to have to deal with things. I didn't want to admit I couldn't cope." Ron held my hand tighter.

"The business was failing, spectacularly. Caitlin's marriage had crumbled and she was in bits. I tried to tell you but, then there was the fire and you lost your job." Ron looked up apologetically. "I'm not blaming you. I just didn't want to put you through all this too."

Ron took another large drink. I hadn't noticed he'd brought the bottle through. What was left of it.

"As soon as I passed David over for promotion you knew something was up." Ron looked at me, melting my anger again and again.

"If I was going to prison I could at least make sure he wasn't. Brian had experience with this kind of thing before. He's officious, you hate him but we were in a bloody big hole and, as far as I could see, he was the only one who could get us out of it. Then, he started seeing Neil."

"Neil?" I laughed. I couldn't help it. "Neil's mystery man is Brian?"

"I thought you knew."

No wonder he thought I'd be angry. Having it away with the Bulldog. That's practically bestiality. There had to be laws against that kind of thing and, if there weren't, there should be.

Is that why Neil thought the mysery man took the CCTV? Was that a good enough reason? Ron knew about the relationship and Brian didn't give a shit what I thought.

"I don't think Brian wanted me to know. I don't think Brian wanted anyone to know. It wasn't right, Jen. The way he hid Neil away." The compassion still there in his voice.

David hadn't understood either; Ron hadn't devalued him. He had tried to protect him.

"I thought if I could just get to New York." Ron kept talking, "The lawyers and the accountants there would figure it out. it. The more we investigated things here the worse it all got. But the moment you hung up the phone I realised. If this is the end Jen, I want to spend it with you."

The reality of the situation hung between us. Ron could go to jail.

All these months and I'd failed to notice. This wasn't my Armageddon. It was his.

CHAPTER 51

I thought it was me. I thought I was the curse that brought the lives of all those around me hurtling towards the sun. Turns out we're all fairly adept at hitting the self-destruct button.

"It's ok." I said what everyone wants to hear at the lowest point.

"We'll get through this. I promise."

I wouldn't leave Ron. I couldn't now. We didn't need to think about the future. We just had to manage the now.

"Start at the beginning." I had to remain focused. He'd tried to tell me before but my mind wandered off. This time the hamster wouldn't juggle but, there was something else gnawing at my brain. Something important. Something demanding my attention. Something about My Own Little Personal Armageddon.

"It was back in March ...."

Was it advice? Something comforting I wanted to say? At the height of my crisis when everyone told me it was 'all going to be ok in the end' I'd laughed. Well, not exactly laughed. I had wanted to punch them.

273

"There were a couple of disproportionate pay-outs across the country. Birmingham, Bradford, Manchester, Wales."

Wales is a separate country but, ok, not the time.

There was something about those place names.

Stop humming Jen.

"New buildings, not up to speck, and disproportionate insurance claims pay outs."

Fireman Sam's words echoed in my ears, 'shouldn't have gone up that quick'. Something about the Leisure Centre not being up to specification. The plans not matching the end result.

Stay focused, Jen. This isn't about you.

The damn picture of the ATM distracted me again. The infernal song Neil and I had devised played on repeat in my head.

"Insurance claims for what?" I spoke over the internal din.

There was something about the place names. The list Ron had just mentioned. Like, it was in the wrong order.

"Fires mostly." Ron began picking at his nail beds.

I held his hand to prevent him any more discomfort. "How much money."

"Hundreds of thousands." Ron's head flopped forward; as if he no longer had the strength to hold himself up in the world. "It could even be millions."

Sums of money so large they were incomprehensible.

Fire! That was it. Ron had told me at my lowest point I was a phoenix. A creature that had to be consumed by fire to rise again; bolder, stronger, better. I should tell him that.

It's not that.

"That's when I brought in Brian. He had experience of investigating 'inside jobs'. I got him to go through the accounts but, it just kept getting worse. He found large sums of money were missing." Ron put his head in his hands. He was exhausted, broken.

"Inside jobs?" I thought of all the screw ups I had been responsible for at Smiths. Even I had to conceded this level of incompetence was beyond even me.

"You think someone at Smiths is involved in this?" There were a sea of faces; not all of them known. I wondered how you would ever narrow it down.

"It's not just human error?" People make mistakes.

"This is proper, criminal activity." Ron looked defeated.

"David would have noticed." The one thing I had learned at Smiths was that everyone else seemed pretty competent. "Someone would have caught this. Ron, this doesn't make any sense."

There were fires and insurance claims but, there also seemed to be embezzlement.

Ron was too close to see it.

Carol's voice echoed in my head. 'You see things that other people don't. It just takes you a while to figure out what's important'.

"They think someone starts the fires and ...."

"Bloody hell!" I leapt off the bed. "It's not about the phoenix!"

CHAPTER 52

The fire. That's what was gnawing at my brain. The list of places Ron had reeled off echoed Chris's LinkedIn Profile. The inspiration for Neil and I's Proclaimer's mash up. All the places Ron had named Chris had worked in some trumped-up nonsense job in each of the Councils. That's how I knew the fires were in Aberystwyth. It didn't fit the tune; it didn't scan. Neil and I had tried for weeks but the Proclaimers had steered clear of any Welsh sounding towns.

It's a coincidence.

It can't be.

I threw the melted pencil case into a heap of clothes on the floor and stuck my memory stick into Ron's computer.

"Have we been robbed?" Ron surveyed Joey's trail of destruction in our flat. Now we were both home it was ridiculous to think he'd ever be gone.

"Have you been sleeping on the sofa?" I heard the tears again in his voice.

"I don't know about you but I haven't exactly been sleeping."

277

Ron held me again. Sometimes there were just no words.

"This has been the worst week of my life." Ron's voice full of emotion. "I'm lost without you, Jen. I promise you, whatever happens, things are going to change. I will never neglect you again."

"You're damn right things are going to change." The document I had been searching for flashed up on the screen. Good old Elsa, protecting my memory stick from those wicked flames.

"After my little Armageddon I was taking no chances. Look." I pushed the laptop towards Ron. He hadn't exactly been overjoyed when I'd interrupted his heartfelt confession back in Cailtin's spare room. "It's always about the footnotes."

Caitlin's spare room. I had already given Ron's flat to her.

Ron scanned the document. "The Community Centre was underwritten by Smiths. Well, this is going to look bloody great in court!"

"It went on fire in June. Just after Chris took over."

Ron failed to see the significance.

"Chris worked in all of those towns you mentioned." I pulled up his profile page.

"They arrested Mac." Ron scanned the information on the screen as his forehead creased. The lines had become more entrenched.

"Mac couldn't start a sentence never mind a fire."

Ron looked disappointed. "This won't be enough."

278

He was trying to be nice. Trying to pretend he didn't think I was bat shit crazy.

"This policy starts in April. Before that the insurance was much smaller, look." I showed him the old policy.

Chris had tried to sneak it past us all as his unique contribution to the new made-up job; better insurance. It was a crappy little Community Centre in a rundown part of town; but, it was also mine.

"There was something bugging me back at the flat."

"Caitlin?" He almost smiled.

"I was reading your boring magazines."

Ron grinned.

"Fine! I was looking at the pictures. Right at the back was an image of an ATM.

Ron continued to look blank.

"A cash point." I offered.

"I know what an ATM is, Jen."

"Remember all those muggings near the Centre? They put CCTV up at the cash point and those cameras are right opposite the centre!"

CHAPTER 53

"It should have been destroyed by rights." The Desk Sergeant took Ron and I through to the back of the Police station. "Someone noticed the date and held onto it but, the images are too grainy."

Showing us the CCTV footage of the night of the fire probably broke all kinds of rules and regulations. Maybe a couple of laws too. Like half the population though the copper recognised Ron. He perhaps recognised too my determination. I wasn't going to leave without seeing that footage.

The video was very poor quality. A hooded figure leapt over the wall and ran towards the Community Centre. A few seconds later smoke wafted past the screen and the cash point glowed red, reflecting the flames.

I watched the disappointment in their faces and acknowledged Carol was right; I didn't suffer from a lack of attention. I was gifted with an abundance of it. My super brain was very quick to detect what many must have dismissed before me. Ron and the Desk Sergeant had watched the same short clip and they had been looking in all the wrong places.

"It went up quick." Ron regained the power of speech. "It was a good try." He tried to mask the disappointment.

The Sergeant nodded sympathetically but subtly checked his watch.

"Neither of you thought that was at all helpful or illuminating?"

The Sergeant looked at Ron in a plea to take the mad woman home.

"I can deduce two things." I sounded like one of those TV cops. Maybe there would be a documentary about it. I wondered who would play me.

Jen! Focus!

"Firstly, the fact that the Police thought a man known locally as Hippy Crack Mac because of his penchant for the sweet lady H."

"None of those drug references are correct." The Sergeant looked disappointed.

"Have you ever seen a drug addict run like that? With such speed and precision? And, I don't mean professional athletes."

I nodded to the screen. "Roll it back a few seconds."

The Sergeant did as I requested.

"Look at the size of the figure compared to that bin. That's not Mac. Whoever this is he's at least a foot shorter than Mac."

The Sergeant quickly reviewed the tape.

"That gets Mac off the hook." Ron beamed. "You have to send this to Peter."

"Peter?" I felt a lump in my throat. "You assigned one of your legal team to Mac? In the midst of all of this?"

How could I have ever doubted Ron's integrity?

"All this proves is Mac didn't start the fire." Ron frowned. "We already knew that."

"How did *we* know that?"

Ron looked as though it was evident. "You said."

My word had been enough.

"Do you want to know who did?" I teased.

That was the second thing I spotted in the clip. The inspiration of the bins had come later. When my super brain rewound the footage in my head.

"He's about forty years old. Sure he'll claim he's twenty-seven but he's a tool, and you shouldn't believe a word he says. He's of athletic build, 5 foot 7. Well, five foot three but he wears inserts. I suspect he uses Botox."

"Anything else?" The Sergeant seemed far less impressed with that analysis.

"He is one of the worst human beings you're ever likely to meet. Honestly, billions of people on this planet and that's my guess at the worst." I tapped the screen. "An utter confidence trickster who'd do literally anything." Even poor Neil.

"You can't tell all that from the video." The Sergeant harrumphed. My initial finding had given him false hope of a speedy conviction.

"No." I pointed to the frozen image on the screen. "But what I can tell you is that's the wonderful Brian's shagging wagon."

How the 'investigation' had failed to identify a brand new Lotus parked in the most deprived part of town on the night of an arson attack wasn't in the least bit suspicious was beyond me.

CHAPTER 54

"This is why you are one of my heroes." Carol beamed. "I want to be like you when I grow up."

"Say that in front of a witness."

"Never." She smiled as the music blared behind us.

Mum whispered to the DJ to turn it down. Dad growled at him to turn it off.

"You said you loved me." I sang along to the tune.

"Piss off, Jen. So, what are we calling this?" Carol looked around the collection of our nearest and dearest. "The we're not going to jail party?"

"Is this the part when I'm supposed to claim it was nothing and be all modest?"

Neil and I had inadvertently cracked the case. Our memorial song for Chris needed a new verse. I sang: "When you go, won't you send me, a Postcard from the Penitentiary."

Carol looked at me thoughtfully. "You know Jen, you don't really need to have faith in Stephen, or Ron, or anyone else. You just need to have faith in yourself." The only thing more impressive than your screw-ups are the come-backs."

"This wasn't my screw up." I reminded her. Although, I had to acknowledge there was a lot about the past few weeks that I could have done different. A lot I would be doing differently in the future.

"And, it was nothing." I feigned humility.

"Caitlin told me Brian and Chris were doing the nasty."

"That's a mental image that'll last."

"Then, Ron said it was Neil and Brian." I presented the evidence as it had come to me.

"Not Ron and Brian then." Carol mocked.

"Neil said he and the mystery man were at the Community Centre the night of the fire." I ignored the provocation. "Neil thought MM had taken the CCTV. Then, he'd ditched him. I just thought they were up to some seriously kinky stuff but, no. Brian took the CCTV because he planned from the very start to burn the Community Centre to the ground. For the insurance. Brian used Neil."

"Chris had been involved in the drafting of the plans for the Centre. He cut corners and he pocketed the money that saved." They had some kind of scam with the insurance claim too. Full disclosure, the hamster started to juggle when that bit was explained.

"Bulldog Brian and Neurotic Neil." Carol shook her head. "No wonder Neil thought you would hate him."

"I think it was more that he hated himself."

We'd invited Neil to the party. I hoped he would come.

285

"Brian burnt the Community Centre down." Carol found it hard to believe the well-groomed man in the designer suit was capable of it.

"The Police think that's how they got away with it for so long. They kept it just the pair of them. The fewer people who were involved the less fault lines. Until the stupid prick parked his flash car in sight of the CCTV." I laughed.

It was only slightly less competent than the guy I'd read about who had robbed and bank then got them to deposit the money in his account.

Carol watched as Neil paced outside the door.

"How it looks from the outside of a relationship isn't always how it feels from the inside."

"Wow." Carol raised her glass. "She finally gets it."

"Neil thought Brian loved him."

A moment of silence passed as a marker of respect. I watched as Ron went outside into the rain the encourage Niel inside. Neil flew into his arms.

"Wow." Carol sneered. "Can't you just feel the sexual tension?"

I wouldn't be provoked.

"The Police think they made millions out of this scam. Brian got cocky. He was the one skimming money from Smiths."

I felt more than a bit of relief at that. My job there was supposed to have something to do with invoices. I wasn't as confident as Ron, David and Janice that the whole thing couldn't have actually been my fault.

"Chris set up the insurance scam and Brian worked it all from the inside." I wasn't entirely sure what either of them did but from the reactions of all in the room when Ron explained it was Hell of an illegal.

"That explained why Chris kept hanging around Woodfield and why it was almost in his interest that it failed."

Apparently it explained too why Chris kept hanging around after the fire; he had misplaced the original insurance. The one that demonstrated the Centre had been worth more to the Council intact that reduced to a pile of ash. I prided myself on being so forward thinking. That, and the copy of the document he spent months trying to find, had long ago been consigned (by me) to confidential waste.

"I wouldn't have put Brian and Chris together as a couple either. Proper Bonnie and Clyde routine." Carol frowned.

I watched as Neil continued to hover at the door. "You weren't the only one."

CHAPTER 55

"Dad said you were amazing." Caitlin choked the words out. At least, she pretended to. Much of the venom she had for me was gone.

"In keeping your child alive or sorting out the whole impending doom?"

"Both." Caitlin tried to make it sound like grudging praise as she put her cocktail menu down.

"We didn't get a chance to talk after." She paused. "What I told you at the hospital."

Caitlin was reimagining the whole incident as her near brush with death. There would be several life searching moments and spiritual enlightenments to come. Caitlin and Mum had been talking excitedly for the past half hour. Caitlin had been describing walking towards a light. Light felt unlikely. Flames I could get on board with.

"You look amazing." Praise where it was due.

Caitlin's hair and make-up had been professionally done. Just like Janice. They'd had a wonderful half hour chat about that. In this light, and with these people, Caitlin still looked almost human.

"I think you have a new fan there." Mum raised her eyebrows as she went in search of Dad. He'd been bestowing on Ron the virtues of WD40 the last time I'd seen them.

Ron may have been forgiven for the recent heartache he had caused his daughter but the poor DIY and home maintenance was an ongoing and unresolved issue. It was amazing for Dad that my life was back on track but, he could not so easily forget the trauma of the squeaky hinges.

Mum had given up on the old Judaism for now and is part of a local neighbourhood UFO watch. Well, I say local but she has to travel to the next village to get a better class of nut job. Honestly, you couldn't make it up.

"You know Caitlin, from here on in you don't have to like me but, you do have to show me some respect." Ron had not been the only one to let Caitlin walk all over me.

Caitlin sat back, impressed. "I like you Jen, and I'm not just saying that because I'm compromised."

There were so many words I would have chosen for Caitlin a few days ago. Compromised wasn't one of them.

"I wouldn't blame you if you told Craig." Caitlin lowered her voice as Mum moved away.

Craig was at the bar. The hospital incident had 'put things in perspective' and they were 'looking to reconcile'. Seemed good timing given Ron wasn't going

289

to jail and was back in the black. I hoped Caitlin realised she deserved better. I obviously couldn't tell her that.

"You deserve better. Not much like, but a bit better."

Hey, turns out I could.

For a moment Caitlin looked vulnerable again.

"It was a long and emotional night. I don't remember everything that happened at the hospital. Other than that it was the beginning of my superhero status. I remember that."

I'd no recollection of the event that was doing the rounds tonight. I hadn't met the priest who had apparently performed the last rites. I'd also apparently missed what must have been a rapid conversion to Catholicism.

"I'd tell if it was you." Caitlin sounded almost convincing.

Last week undoubtedly but this week, I wasn't so sure. We'd be unlikely to ever be best friends but I had the feeling we were no longer enemies. Not because I kept her secret but because I kept her child safe when she couldn't. Even if he might have hepatitis from touching a stranger's piss on a pregnancy stick he'd found in a bin.

It could have been yours.

It's not just that I didn't have the time to pee on a stick (well, if you have time to pee you have time to push a stick in the flow). I just hadn't plucked up the courage to take another test.

"I'd tell him myself." I laughed, unintentionally underlining my inability to keep a secret but I could forget this one.

"I don't have secrets from your Dad though, not anymore. But Craig won't hear it from me."

"Thanks." She looked genuinely relieved. "You know, if you married him" Caitlin pretended to be distracted by her nails . "It wouldn't be the worst thing ever."

"I'm not interested in marrying Craig."

Caitlin scowled.

"I mean, even I can do better."

Caitlin looked at Craig standing at the bar, this time more thoughtfully. "I'm not good on my own."

"You wouldn't be on your own." I'd proven that.

Even when Caitlin hated me I'd helped her. At first because I loved Ron and now, well, I don't mind her. Much.

"Maybe I was a bit jealous." Caitlin laughed and held the menu in front of her impeccable face. It was a genuine laugh; it made her eyes sparkle.

"Don't look at me like that. It's ridiculous. I'm a married woman with my own child for goodness sake. I should not be jealous that my father has attention to give to someone else."

I didn't think it was his attention that she envied. Ron and I were happy. Now, more than ever.

"You don't have to be married." I was going to insist she kept Joey. I had grown quite fond of that little Hellion.

I pushed the menu from her face so I could look her in the eye. "There are worse things than being single."

Craig returned to the table as if on cue. I made a sharp exit. His hand had 'accidentally' grazed my butt twice already.

"Things seem to be going better." Stephen handed me a glass of champagne.

Ron had booked the bar for the evening for our nearest and dearest to celebrate. Of course Stephen had to be the waiter. No-one had thought to check.

"I'm sorry I was weird with you. I wanted to be ok about you being married and about to have kids but, I didn't know how to feel. Maybe it's always just going to be weird."

Ron looked over and smiled. I mean, he could be a little jealous.

I had told Ron about the unexpected encounters with Stephen. I explained where I was the night I had lied and said I was at my parents. Ron had told me where he was other than the gym. 'Work, Jen. Trying to make sure we didn't all end up in prison.' I'd just beamed triumphantly. 'You should have looped me in earlier.' Ron had laughed, with a proper smile that went all the way to his eyes. 'I'll know better for next time.' You see, we all make mistakes. We just have to learn from them.

"You ok?" Ron mouthed. I nodded and smiled. More than ok. I was again complete.

Ron had never even crossed the door of the study since he'd returned from New York. He'd already promised to take me wherever I wanted for a holiday. Right now, all I wanted was here.

"Maybe it just takes time." Stephen looked jealous. He had no right to be, but it felt awkward having them both here.

I knew this would be the last time that I saw Stephen. Our final meeting. The lesson was now complete.

I watched Ron hand Neil a drink and with a hug he welcomed him back into the fold.

"You asked what made Ron and I different to us." I suddenly understood. "We can't stay broken up."

Stephen smiled, but sadly this time.

"I really do wish you well." And, at least part of me meant it.

CHAPTER 56

"You look amazing." Neil was genuinely relieved to see me look more like my old self.

"Well, you know, I finally had to shave my legs as I didn't have time to brush out the matted hair. Thank the Time Lord you've lost the frosted tips."

Neil too looked better. Still thin but, clean at least.

"I should have told you it was Brian." Neil shifted his weight awkwardly from one leg to the other.

"Then, I wouldn't have thought you were shagging Ron."

"You thought what?" Neil almost spat his drink out.

"I was having a little mental breakdown."

"A little?" Neil laughed.

"Are you saying you don't find my boyfriend attractive?"

Neil placed the glass down to avoid any further incidents. "I would have sex with Ron in a heartbeat but, sisters before misters, right?"

"Right." No man would come between us again.

"Brian was with Chris on a Tuesday and a Thursday." Neil glanced away, as though it was unimportant.

"I figured." It had been a Tuesday night in the cafe. Chris had looked dishevelled but my brain hadn't allowed me to see it at the time. Apparently they were mega into clubbing and drugs. That explained the wild look in his eyes.

"I thought amphetamines made you thin." Neil still sounded hurt. It would take time.

"Might be an idea." The new dress I had bought for the party already felt constricted.

"It won't always feel like this." I tried to sound all sage like his inspirational calendar. "This too shall pass. It'll pass like a bloody kidney stone but, it'll pass."

I hugged him too.

"All that time we spent with Coronary Chris we didn't know anything about him." Neil wiped his eyes. I pretended not to notice his tears. So many emotions in such little drops.

"We didn't want to know him."

"If only he wasn't a dreadful criminal, we could have learnt a powerful lesson." Neil smiled.

"I would like to know how he's going to fare in prison. He's going to hate the coffee!" I laughed.

"If it helps I'm not sure he and Brian really loved each other. I think it was more, just, well, convenient." I had no idea what passed between them but, I thought that might be easier for Neil to tolerate.

"I thought he liked me." Neil whispered, almost to himself.

"Maybe he did." I looked back at Stephen serving drinks. Mum told me he'd be moving out of the city to find a larger house. The twins would be arriving soon. Stephen had another a job at another bar to save money on travel.

"Maybe he loved you, in his own way."

CHAPTER 57

"Do you want to dance, Ms. Blake?" Ron held out his hand.

"No one else is dancing."

"We could start a trend." He pulled me closer and we swayed in time to the music.

"Do you remember when I thought you were gay?"

It had been a fleeting hypothesis that Neil's mystery man was Ron.

"Was it just work?" I hadn't wanted to ask. All the nights in the study. The distance that had grown between us.

Ron seemed anxious to offer up another confession. I hoped it would be his last. "When I left with the gym bag I wanted you to think that's where I was going but sometimes, I went to physiotherapy. The knee is getting worse."

"Did the physio help?"

"I suppose."

It didn't sound like it helped.

"I was embarrassed."

"To be taking care of your medical needs?" I thought of the unused pregnancy test. I could force Janice and Caitlin into the toilet to stand watch. That's the kind of thing people did, wasn't it?

"I was embarrassed of being old."

"You're not old." I leaned in closer. "You're just older than me."

It was reality. There was nothing we could do to change it.

"The doctor said I'll need a knee replacement."

"My bionic man." I smiled. "I can use that to my advantage. If you try and disappear into the study I'll buy an industrial magnet and drag you back out."

Ron laughed and leaned in closer. "We can board up the door to that bloody cupboard."

"We can't. I'm going to use it for shoes."

"What were you and Caitlin talking about?" Ron looked anxiously at Caitlin. Checking for a pencil in the eye no doubt.

"We've been having an affair. Now we've stitched up Brian and Chris we're wondering what to do with the loot."

Ron shrugged. "I'd just be relieved you were getting on." He smiled.

"I'll tell you later." We'd have no secrets now. Not even this one. Ron had learnt his lesson and I had learnt mine. I'm bloody brilliant under pressure.

CHAPTER 58

So, there we have it. Two Little Armageddons later and we were back on top of the world. The Council had offered me all manner of jobs to 'make up for the stress and misunderstandings'. They said, on reflection, 'I was one of the best employees they'd ever had'. I'd retorted that given the current situation, and reputation of the council, that was like saying I was the best arsonist in the room. No one laughed. Too soon, right?

I'd put it in words even they could understand. There was a 'lack of goodness of fit' between me and the hum drum council machine. So, once again I was afloat on the sea of possibilities. Paddling like hell and struggling to keep my head above water? Not this time. For the first time in my life I was able to tolerate uncertainty. I didn't really know what I wanted to do but that was ok, I didn't have to. Life could be uncertain and Ron and I could manage that together.

I probably should be a motivational speaker. Having survived my own Little Personal Armageddon and heroically saved Ron from his I had a lot to teach the world but, I had to accept maybe the world wasn't ready to hear it.

Five days apart had been a potent reminder of the life I didn't want; existence without Ron. We'd taken another step down commitment highway. Ron had signed his flat over to Caitlin. He wanted her to have 'options' (namely to leave Creepy Craig). Ron's name was added to my mortgage; I joked that he wanted me to have less options. The flat was officially ours. As it had always been. It felt like a risk but, what's life without risk? You can't wrap yourself up in a little protective bubble because once upon a time you were hurt. Also, Peter set me up with a cracking contract that heavily favoured me if Ron and I ever separated. At least, that's Peter told me. It turns out it covered all kinds of eventualities but the outcome of each was the same; I was financially secure.

'You'd better pay your share of the mortgage in used non-sequential notes.' I'd quipped, making the solicitor even more uncomfortable when we signed the mountain of paperwork. Our solicitor was a lovely woman with a fine attention to detail but, he-haw social skills and zero sense of humour.

'Have you ever thought about a career in HR?' I'd offered. Smiths was back on the up. Employees were returning, even more were needed.

David had, of course, taken his rightful place as Ron's second in command.

"Is there anything else you want to tell me?" Ron's eyes widened at the news his daughter had been having an affair, and I'd alluded as discretely as I could, to the fact this may be an inherited maternal trait.

I could tell from Ron's tone he had known, or at least suspected, what I had told him.

"In case I haven't mentioned it lately Mr. Smith, I really do love you."

Ron leaned in closer and kissed me.

No longer afraid of public displays of affection; perhaps that had all been in my head too.

"I promise you, Jen. I won't screw things up again."

"Of course you will." I laughed. "We're both going to bungle along buggering this up for the rest of our lives. But there's no one else I'd rather screw it all up with."

"Me neither."

"I'm glad you're not going to prison."

"Me too." The relief was evident on Ron's face. It was evident on David's and Janice's too. Thankfully, my whole social circle seemed to be drinking a lot less Brandy.

"I'm glad too that I don't have to spend my Sundays heading to the Big House on the Bang Bus."

"What's the Bang Bus?"

"I saw it on Netflix. It's a bus that takes you for conjugal rights in prison."

Ron laughed. "I think that's only in America and, I think the bus is just for prison transport."

"You didn't see the documentary." I mocked; as though I had a greater understanding of the American penitentiary system.

"I need a new job." I said it without the same frustration but, I think I had almost completed every box set on every streaming channel now.

"You could offer me a job at Smiths? I did save the company."

"Never." He shook his head. "You were one of the worst employees I ever had."

"But since Brian, not the actual worst. Right? Maybe I should head-up recruitment. You let me and Brian slip through the net. That's a dodgy net."

"Well, you'd have time to retrain now that you don't have to spend all your weekends on the bus. I think you have to be married for those kinds of rights, anyway." He tried to sound casual.

I still hadn't answered his question.

"Well," I smiled, playfully. "Peter is all about future proofing. So, if it secures my seat on the bus then I'd probably be up for marriage."

Ron took me in his arms and kissed me with a passion that had never been seen outside the confines of our little flat. Or the shower cubicle in Pulling the Plug. Maybe we'd have our engagement and wedding party there. Just for the bants.

Everyone we knew and loved was gathered here and Ron didn't care. Of all our unbearably happy traits we'd just added public displays of affection (and PTSD for

Caitlin) to the list. This really was a new beginning. The new Jen was going to be stronger, wiser, and more focused. She would have more faith in herself, and the people she loved. The new Jen was going to rock it.

As we raised our glass to toast the future for the first time in months, I had an appetite for alcohol. Perfect timing when there was an abundance of champagne. I'd only just brought the cold, delicious glass to my lips when suddenly and unmistakably the stomach flu kicked.

Gillian Lee *Gibson is a self-published author. A Bump in the Road* is the sequel to her debut novel *My Own Little Personal Armageddon.*

Gillian has a growing collection of darker tales. Her psychological thriller, *Shore Gulls*, is complete and awaiting publication. Gillian is completing her first crime novel, *Dark Angel.*

Gillian has a background in Religious, Moral and Philosophical Studies and currently works as a Psychologist. Gillian draws from this experience and brings a deep understanding of human behaviour and questions of morality to her work.

Please visit Gillian's author's page to keep updated on her recent work.

amazon.com/author/gillian_lee_gibson

My Own Little
Personal
Armageddon
Gillian Lee Gibson

Printed in Dunstable, United Kingdom